THE DISCUS THROWERS

Tom Wakefield's other books include the novels *Mates*, *Trixie Trash Star Ascending*, *Isobel Quirk in Orbit*, *The Love Siege*; the collection of short stories *Drifters*; and his childhood autobiography *Forties Child*.

TOM WAKEFIELD
THE DISCUS THROWERS

First published in October 1985 by GMP Publishers Ltd
PO Box 247, London N15 6RW, England

Second impression August 1988

British Library Cataloguing in Publication Data

Wakefield, Tom
The discus throwers.
I. Title
823'.914[F]   PR6073.A374

ISBN 0–907040–80–2
ISBN 0–907040–79–9 Pbk

Typeset by Wilmaset, Birkenhead, Wirral L41 1HB
Printed in the European Community
by Norhaven A/S, Viborg, Denmark

for
Valerie Hand
Robert Collie
and
Francis King

And I have recognised your courage amongst the other qualities. For me it has been a strange evening, with its stirring up of the past, and its foreshadowing of things that may even touch the future. It has almost seemed incongruous on the day of parting.

Ivy Compton-Burnett
A Father and his Fate

I have learned the universal language, and I know that all living things will find their intercourse not in joint obedience to the laws of science, not in the chance identity of a passion or a function, but in the gradual discovery that though they traverse different paths the same thing lies at the goal of all their desire.

E. M. Forster
Simply the Human Form

One

Betty Hooper paused for a moment before she crossed the road. This was not from shortage of breath or on account of passing traffic. This particular road was closed to all vehicles. She had merely stopped to think.

She reflected that this was to be her last week in the job that she had pursued for all her working life. This was her last week of teaching, and unlike many teachers she enjoyed her work. She had never been ambitious. As far as she was concerned scale posts were just a matter of patronage and nothing to do with extra effort. Now, three years before her retirement age she had acquiesced and opted for an early retirement with a reduced pension. Her present head-teacher, Mrs Goodheart, had left Betty little choice.

Betty was no masochist and the daily subtle sadisms that Mrs Goodheart had perpetrated on her for the past three years had finally broken Betty's will. Fortunately, Betty's heart was void of rancour and she was not a person to indulge in self-pity; she strode forward and was sorry to disturb the city pigeons pecking at the pavement and gutter. They flew all about her head, anxious and disgruntled.

The school building was situated in what could once have been a small reservoir or a large well. It was much below ground level and although the building itself was two-storeyed it had the appearance of looking like a bungalow built by some eccentric millionaire. Even the wire-netting fixed over the window-panes did not look out of place. The school were at play taking their lunch break. There did not appear to be many children about, but what children there were did seem to be exceedingly noisy. She descended the steps and heard a voice say, 'Fuck you, Charles.' The same voice spoke to her in a very friendly way and said: 'Hello, Mrs – er – no – Miss Hooper. Mrs Goodheart wants to see you – there's a note on the notice board. It says, "Will Miss Hooper see me on return." Where have you been, Miss?'

'I've just been doing a little shopping. I've never played truant, Tracy . . .' Before Betty could say any more Tracy had begun to quarrel with Charles.

Betty settled the quarrel by letting the two assailants accompany her to the headmistress's office. Diversion, or early diversion, often ended a fight before it had begun. All wars, singular or collective, seemed to prove this. Betty was a pacifist. By the time that Tracy, Betty and Charles had reached the office all quarrelling had ceased. Charles had ceded that Tracy's current pop idol wasn't a poofter and Tracy had said that she didn't care if he was or not and that he was still great. They left together talking of the popular musical tastes of their parents which provided them with mirth and disbelief rather than discord.

Betty looked at the contraption fixed on the wall outside the office. Before Mrs Goodheart's arrival one had merely knocked on the door. Now a nasty buzzing machine which looked like a miniature traffic-lights was fixed to the wall. There were four buttons: (1) Press. (2) Enter. (3) Engaged. (4) Wait. Betty drove her index finger on to the 'Press' button. It buzzed and a light flickered on the 'Enter' button. She opened the door and managed to take two steps inside the office. She did not receive a greeting from Mrs Goodheart. Quite the opposite. Mrs Goodheart did not speak to her but embarked on a mime that expressed irritation.

Her left hand held the telephone, she pointed to this as if the message she was receiving from it was announcing a nuclear holocaust. Then she pointed at Betty and then pointed at the door; Betty crept out as the gesture was more stentorian than any bellow. She closed the door behind her. The machine buzzed, the lights changed, the two that were now lit up said: 'Engaged – Wait.'

Betty sat on a bench outside the study and waited. The bench was most uncomfortable as she was forced to perch forward by the array of exotic potted plants positioned behind the bench. The bench and the exotic plants were some of Mrs Goodheart's first 'innovations' after her appointment. This had been five years ago. Betty sighed; the previous headteacher, Miss Trask, had placed comfortable chairs where Betty was sitting now. It is true they lacked aesthetic appeal, but at least they were welcoming. Miss Trask was considered to be old-fashioned – even ridiculous in Mrs Goodheart's present vision. The chairs had disappeared under an A.O.B. at Mrs Goodheart's first staff-meeting.

'I'm sure no one will object – I'm having the four armchairs removed from outside my room. It's a luxury which ought not to be on display. I don't know what visitors think when they come here and see those chairs in the corridor. Ah, oh, I think that they might look more suitable in a hotel lounge in Eastbourne. Perhaps that is why some parents appear to malinger in them too long. Why, yesterday, two mothers sat there for quite twenty minutes – just talking – I had seen both of them. They'll be wanting a cup of tea served next. It really isn't for me to comment on the little foibles of my predecessor – but Miss Trask tended to cosset rather than help. The chairs seem to me to be a symbol of wasted expense.' Mrs Goodheart was about to close the meeting. Everyone had been surprised when Betty spoke up.

'The chairs were not an expense. Miss Trask had them delivered from her own home. They cost nothing. She wanted parents to be comfortable.' Betty had blushed – she had rarely spoken at staff-meetings. Mrs Goodheart had stared at her intently; she smiled and decided that Betty would have to go. It would take longer than the armchairs but it could be achieved. The armchairs went within a month. The bench and the plants arrived – the cost of the changes had been met out of the school fund.

The startling buzzer-sound broke Betty's reverie – she started back and fractured an intrusive rubber leaf. It hung pathetically injured from its stem. The buzzing continued and Betty ignored the maimed plant to obey the 'Enter' sign.

Mrs Goodheart had completed her negotiations with the travel agency. She always took a fortnight abroad at Easter. It was to be Corfu this year. She greeted Betty as she always did. It was as though Betty's presence provided constant concern and surprise. 'Ah, Miss Hooper. Sorry to keep you waiting. Had to speak to the D.O. on some urgent admissions – work is never done, is it? There really is no room for a pause in my job. However – pause I must – as I have to have one or two words with you.' An interview with Mrs Goodheart was always made out to be a favour. As if to give strength to her powers of patronage, Mrs Goodheart inspected her clear varnished nails before letting Betty know that it was all right for her to sit down.

'Well, you have four days left with us here – and then – and then – your life as a teacher will be over.'

'I'm not sure about that,' said Betty.

'Miss Hooper, I hope that you are not under the delusion that you may apply for another post. This will not be possible as you have accepted pensionable retirement – and, of course, there is the question of references. I don't think that I could support . . .'

'I won't need any references. I think that my best teaching has been done out of schools rather than in them.' Betty did not want to pursue Mrs Goodheart's well-trodden themes. She wanted the woman to get to the point. Could there be yet another wound that Mrs Goodheart wanted to deliver? She had delivered so many over the past three years. Was there to be a final spear thrust?

'You are quite sure that you are not attending the end of term staff tea? As you are leaving it might be a nice gesture. I always give my staff an end of term tea – as you know. I'm sorry that you never saw fit to attend it before. But I wondered' – here Mrs Goodheart paused to pick an imaginary fleck of dust off a fingernail – 'I wondered if you might attend this one – as it is your last day here. There will be no retirement speeches, I assure you. I always feel that they sound like funeral orations, don't you?'

'I never heard any. I have never heard funeral orations or retirement speeches, so I can't say. I'm sorry I won't be able to come on Friday. Will that be all, Mrs Goodheart?'

'I'm afraid that there is just one – er – small matter. Small but – perhaps delicate. I'm sorry that I have to mention it at this late time in the term and particularly as you are so soon to be leaving us. I certainly don't want to hurt your feelings but I do have to think of other members of staff. Please don't take what I have to say personally – it is merely my duty. Duty lies heavy at times you know, Miss Hooper.'

'I'm sure that it does,' Betty replied. So there was going to be another wound. Betty waited. 'I must not get angry,' she told herself. Mrs Goodheart was not dressed like a sadist – but then she wouldn't be. She was not even capable of inflicting pain truthfully.

'It's about the toilet arrangements,' said Mrs Goodheart sweetly.

'Toilet arrangements?' Betty could not keep the surprise from her voice. Mrs Goodheart was pleased with the modulation in Betty's response. There was just the right amount of concern and alarm. Mrs Goodheart savoured Betty's discomfort for a few moments before she continued.

'The rebuilding programme has been an awful nuisance this term and I'm sorry that our eight women members of staff have all been allocated to just the two toilets until the others are completed. I know it has been most trying for you all. Break times are a bit of a loo conveyor-belt, aren't they?'

'I don't think anyone has complained,' said Betty, who was by now more puzzled than alarmed.

'Complaints come to me, Miss Hooper. And I have to relay one to you. It's about the toilets. Er – er – it would seem that at times, after using the toilet you sometimes leave it with undue haste.'

'I beg your pardon?'

'Oh, I don't mean that you leave it unflushed – or that you leave improperly dressed. No, it's a question of odour, Miss Hooper.'

'Odour!'

'Yes, I hate to be so frank – but you must understand that few of us can rarely smell ourselves. It would seem that the air-fresheners do little to disperse the odour that you leave behind. It's rather bad, I fear. Now, please don't get upset about this – I'm just going to give you a little tip. When you next go into the toilet – take in a box of matches. Before you leave – just strike a match. The brimstone is most effective. Perhaps it's the tablets that you are on that are causing the trouble.'

'I'm not ON any tablets.' Betty stood and made her way towards the door. 'Bitch,' she mused as she grasped the handle.

'What was that, Miss Hooper?'

'I said, "hitch", Mrs Goodheart. Not "bitch" or "witch" or "match" but "hitch". Good-day to you.' Betty closed the door gently behind her as she left the office for the last time.

On the following Friday, Mrs Goodheart visited Betty in her classroom. The children had gone home and Betty was leaving her classroom tidy. She did not believe in untidy exits. She locked the last cupboard and chose to ignore Mrs Goodheart who hovered about her desk.

'I suppose you will miss it all, Miss Hooper?' Mrs Goodheart's enquiry held a trace of hope. Betty turned and placed a bunch of keys on the desk.

'Here are my keys. They are all labelled,' she said.

'Whatever will you do with your time? You're not a gardener, are you? Do you have a garden, Miss Hooper? Any family that might visit you if you are feeling *à seule*? Perhaps you might join one of the senior citizens' interest classes? Do you have any hobbies? Of course, you don't travel, do you?'

Betty ignored the questions. Mrs Goodheart was not remotely interested in anyone else's welfare but her own. Her concern was as postured as her hair-do – never a wisp out of place. Betty took her handbag from the back of the chair and made to leave the room.

'Goodbye, Miss Hooper,' Mrs Goodheart called after her. Betty turned in the doorway; 'You are absurd, Mrs Goodheart.' These were her final words spoken in an institution after a teaching career spanning twenty-six years.

Mrs Goodheart was taken aback. Miss Hooper had left before she could respond. 'I suppose she has gone back to some dreary bed-sitting-room flat with a tiny kitchen. Gone back to a life of domestic solitude.' Miss Hooper was the kind of dreary spinster that lived for her work because she had little else to live for. What a drab creature she was

– and so stubborn. 'Thank God I don't have to face that stubbornness any more. Let her nibble at plain cake in her mouse-hole.' Mrs Goodheart clutched the keys in the palm of her hand and chuckled. She had always viewed Betty's honesty and integrity as stubbornness, as she was herself a dishonest woman. She smiled and nodded her way through the corridors of the school as she returned to her room. The prospect of Betty's loneliness and desolation gave her much satisfaction – much pleasure.

Two

It was not known, either generally or more specifically at her place of work, that Betty had taken rooms in Miss Trask's flat which was situated in a popular and cosmopolitan area of West London. Mrs Goodheart could find very little personal information concerning her predecessor.

Miss Trask had been a most private person. Betty had moved into her friend's flat in order to look after her through what was thought to be a long-term illness. It was short, for within a year Miss Trask had died. The leasehold on her flat had been left to Betty. She also left Betty the care of her bachelor brother Kenneth – he came with the lease. Miss Trask had always said that Kenneth was portable. After a long career in Customs and Excise – he enjoyed retirement in London – in his present surroundings he felt that he was at the crossways of the whole world.

The flat was more like a maisonette than a flat as it consisted of three floors of a large house. Its frontage was taken up by a launderette which was rented out by the landlords each time the short lease ended. The wash-place saw many changes. In the past four years Betty's flat had seen changes, too – or rather, additions. Betty had been left with Kenneth; a year later she had been joined by Bertrand, who had given Miss Trask excellent professional support throughout her illness. Bertrand often had guests who seemed to mean a lot to him for short periods of time.

For a large part of the week Betty usually had three lodgers. She still had a bedroom and a large lounge as her own. The large kitchen-cum-dining room was shared by everyone. Like all good repertory companies the players got on well, helped one another in adversity and produced varied entertainments that were not always seasonable.

Betty was a little perturbed to find a large poster stuck on the small side door which was the entrance to her home. It read: 'NOTHING IS TOO DIRTY FOR US. COMPLETE SERVICE – £1.40.'

Betty felt that it would be necessary for her to have a word with the new manager of the launderette. His advertising had encroached on her territory and heaven knew who might ring the front door bell with a sign like that stuck on it. She would have a cup of tea with Kenneth first and see about the poster later.

Kenneth's long and loyal service in the Customs and Excise had left him with some behavioural legacies. To a very great extent, he was still a creature of habit and order. Routine and ritual were part of his life. Kenneth's timing was superb and he was largely responsible for the minor routines that the household adhered to. Kenneth knew what time people of the household went out and what time they usually came in. He knew who slept late, who rose early, who made the most telephone calls and who drank the most milk.

He even knew who was leaving and entering the house by the way they closed the door behind them. Kenneth's meticulous eye and ear for detail did not always endear him to everyone. But this was an accepting and forgiving domestic world that he was now part of – irritation was usually expressed with raised eyebrows and other signs, rather than spleen. As Kenneth heard the front door close, he switched on the electric kettle. He had already warmed the teapot. Betty liked a cup of tea when she came home from work. No sugar. Just a little milk.

'I hope it is to your liking, Betty.' Kenneth always made this observation when Betty had the cup just a half-centimetre from her lips. She sipped.

'Lovely, lovely. It's lovely, Kenneth. No one makes a cup of tea as you do.' Betty's approval was either 'lovely' or 'perfect' as far as Kenneth's tea was concerned. She did enjoy his ministrations and he enjoyed cosseting her in this manner. 'Well, it's over. I don't have to go into a school anymore.' Betty took a larger second sip of tea and then placed her cup back in the saucer.

'You won't be coming in at ten-past five next Monday, then?' Kenneth sounded disappointed.

'Not from work I won't. But I might be coming in at ten-past five from somewhere else,' said Betty. She had no plans for such timetabling but did not want to upset Kenneth too much. She knew how he hated disruptions to his day. Even when the clocks went forward or backward Kenneth took at least a week to orientate himself. He always felt cheated by change.

'You can always come down from your room for tea anyway,' said Kenneth. 'We oughtn't to give up our afternoon tête-à-tête.'

'Mm – mm –' Betty murmured – well, he'd settled that. And she did enjoy the afternoon tea-sessions. 'Kenneth! *Kenneth!*' Betty snapped as her glance took in Kenneth's right foot as he crossed his legs.

'Yes, dear?'

'I've told you. I've told you before. I don't like you wearing my slippers.'

'Oh, I'm sorry, dear. It was a lapse.' Kenneth tried to sound contrite but could not refrain from glancing at the pink slipper adorned with frivolous blue pom-poms which decorated his foot.

'They're not even your size. Already, I have to shuffle in them as they are too stretched.'

'I suppose you wouldn't let me have these – I could get you another pair. Something more sensible perhaps – something more comfortable?'

'No, Kenneth. I want my own. I don't mind what you wear but please – not my slippers.' Kenneth kicked them off disconsolately. Betty picked them up and stated that she was going to her room for a little rest.

'It's a bit chilly, isn't it?' she declared as she was about to leave the room.

'Oh, I hadn't noticed it.' Kenneth's retort was cold.

Betty left the kitchen already regretting her short-temperedness. She shivered and decided to turn on the central-heating. If Kenneth was going to sit around in the baby-doll pale lemon nightie for another half-hour then it ought to be a bit warmer for him. She didn't want him to catch pneumonia. His fishnet tights could hardly keep the draughts away.

She lay on her divan, placed two cushions under her head and picked up her history book. She enjoyed reading history books – this particular one was concerned with the lives of Victorian working women. It was full of facts and details. How could the Victorian era be referred to as 'golden'? Betty shook her head as she looked at the numbers of women who had died in childbirth and cruel backstreet abortions. And what of their children? She felt fortunate; half-closed the book and noticed her slippers. They had been a gift from a child. A Christmas present that did not suit. Perhaps, they did look better on Kenneth – would it be wrong to pass a gift on? If Kenneth really liked them – if he needed them . . . then . . . Betty had closed her eyes and entered a guilt-free nap.

She was awakened by the sound of the front doorbell. Her slumber had been deep but short, yet Betty could not rouse herself quickly as sleep had eradicated time, and her fifteen-minute nap could have been eight hours as far as she was concerned. She stretched and yawned. Someone else must have gone to the door – her glass of water – drat – she had left it in the kitchen. Betty felt weary; she raised herself from the divan and pushed her feet into her slippers. Then she patted her hair. She could hear loud noises from the hallway. It sounded like some kind of quarrel.

'There is no music teacher here. I do assure you that none of the people living in this house plays an instrument of any kind. Now, will you please take your foot off this doorstep and go away.' Betty paused on the landing; Kenneth sounded very indignant. Who on earth was he talking to?

'Come on, now. I want just twenty minutes of ball-room dancing. How about a military two-step? I like a strict tempo. A very strict tempo. You could handle it for a tenner. I must say, you look a bit rough – but it's not your face I'm interested in. Go on, I'll make it £15 for a strict *paso doble*. Eh?'

'If you do not remove yourself from this front door in one minute . . .'

Betty hastened down the stairs and grabbed the motor-bike helmet that hung on one of the hall pegs. She jammed it over her head and joined Kenneth in the doorway. She pushed past Kenneth and confronted a man who wore some kind of security guard uniform. 'I'm afraid that you must have the wrong address; this poster refers to the launderette next door.' Betty tore the sign from her front door. 'Although, there seems to be a slight misunderstanding, as I don't believe they teach music there.'

The security guard looked from Betty's crash helmet to Kenneth's fishnet tights. He scratched his head but removed his foot from inside the door. 'But, er – what – what – er?'

'Ah, I can see we have confused you. It's a fancy dress party for senior citizens. We have to have our bit of fun, you know. Innocent – but nice for a laugh when you're over sixty. I'm a thing from outer space.' The man seemed satisfied with this explanation and turned as if to leave, then paused, and added hopefully,

'What about *that* number, then?' He nodded towards Kenneth.

'Number? Number?' Kenneth roared indignantly.

'Oh, he's, he's . . .' Betty coughed for inspiration: 'Ahem . . . ahem . . . he's Titania. Yes, he's Titania. We are both outside time and space. That is our connection. Good-day.' Betty closed the door.

'Really, Betty, if you fell over wearing that crash helmet the weight of it would break your neck. Let me help you off with it. I can't think how you would want to put such a thing on your head in the first place.' Kenneth prized the helmet from its wobbly moorings and placed it back on the hall-peg. They returned to the kitchen for another cup of tea and Betty gave Kenneth her slippers. He accepted them formally as though he were receiving an income-tax rebate. He reminded her they were dining out at 7.30 p.m. This was his treat to her on her retirement from the working world. It was also his way of informing her that he was going to change into what might be considered as more formal attire.

Betty decided that she would wallow in the bath for half an hour before changing her clothes for her dinner date. Her lodgers had decorated the bathroom in black and white. On one wall a six-foot cut-out of a naked male dived upwards as though he were entering infinity. As the taps ran and the steam rose it seemed as though the figure was floating through the clouds. Betty took off her dressing-gown and let the steam whirl around her own thin and wrinkled body. She had lost one breast through illness. She had felt a lump there one day – and four days later the lump was gone, but so was her left breast. She was glad of the steam; it blurred her vision and she was not able to see the scarred tissue.

Betty tested the water with the back of her hand. Just right. Ah, she must remember to put some of the bath oil in the water. Bertrand had bought it for her – her lodgers often bought her presents. She looked at the dark green liquid. The sales blurb said that it would bring all the mysteries of the sea-shore to her bath. Betty paused with the bottle – there were mysteries of the sea-shore like crabs, stinging starfish and barnacles that she would rather not have about her in the bath. She dismissed these irksome creatures from her mind and poured out double the quantity suggested.

Betty settled herself gently beneath the dark blue foaming water. The vapour was indeed pleasing and in spite of her realistic nature Betty thought of the seaside. She did not transport herself to the French Riviera or some exotic Greek Island. Her thoughts took her to Morecambe Pier. She sat on a deck chair next to Miss Trask. Miss Trask had been advised to convalesce in order to prepare for a second abdominal operation. The first had not been successful. Morecambe had been her choice and Betty had gone along with it. The day had been warm, the sun shone; they both wore straw hats and sucked orange juice through a straw out of plastic cartons.

'My dear Betty, I hadn't realised that the sea could go so far out. Really, I'm not sure that I can even see it.' Miss Trask had shielded her eyes with her hand and peered out. 'There is so much sand, so much sand. It's more like sitting on the edge of the Sahara Desert, isn't it? If I stare long enough I might see a mirage.'

'You might give yourself a headache, too. Why don't you put your sunglasses on? They will lower some of the glare,' Betty had said.

'Ah, Betty, you are so thoughtful.' Miss Trask took her sunglasses from her handbag but chose not to look for a mirage. She fell back in her deckchair as though she were in some kind of swoon.

'Mm-mm-mm. I can smell the sea, though. Yes, Betty, I can smell the sea.'

'I think it's shrimps. I think it's shrimps on the stall that you can smell.' Betty had not wanted to wound Miss Trask's romantic train of thought. 'Of course, the shrimps do smell of the sea. They bring the sea with them,' she had added.

Conversation had stopped and Betty began to wonder if she had been reasonable – and then Miss Trask had spoken out into the air, using dreamy tones that Betty had not heard her use before.

'Betty – Betty, my dear. Have you – have you ever known a man?'

'Why, of course I have. I have known, and for that matter still know quite a number of men.' Betty wondered if Miss Trask had caught the sun.

'No, no, I don't think you understand. I mean *known*. I mean "known" in the biblical sense of the word – you know, "she hath known him". Have you? Have you known a man?'

'No, I have not. I don't think a man ever wanted to "know" me – in the biblical sense.' Betty had spoken sharply.

'Did you want to "know" a man,' Miss Trask had persisted.

'No, I did not. I have "known" no one,' Betty had snapped. 'Have you "known" anyone?'

'Yes, yes, I have,' Miss Trask had answered.

'Well, I'm not shocked. If it pleased you both, then it was good,' Betty had said.

'Oh, it pleased us both. It pleased us greatly. But I did not "know" a man. I "knew" a woman. Now, I am sure that I have shocked you. Yes, I "knew" a woman. We savoured each other. It was a long time ago but the memory of it is quite distinct, it must be the ozone. I'm sorry if I have shocked you – but the thought of it all, after all this time, has given me so much pleasure. I shouldn't have mentioned it. I'm sorry.'

'Miss Trask, I am not at all shocked or upset. I'm glad for you – glad that you have known physical love. I have not known it – but if I had I would have entered it.'

'You don't think that it was unnatural of us?'

'If it was unnatural to you both how could it have been done?'

'You are so wise, Betty – and so forthright and tender . . .' Miss Trask had continued. She knew that Betty received compliments with difficulty. 'I'll get us another orange drink and perhaps we could share a bag of shrimps.'

Later, they had wandered to the end of the pier. An aged D.J. was playing old-time dance records. Most of the dancers were over fifty. They drifted through waltzes and attempted some stately quick-steps. They were most courteous with one another. Some spectators might have found this spectacle funny or absurd. Betty had found it charming. She and Miss Trask had smiled at one another – and then had taken to the dance floor and embarked on three waltzes with one another.

In between one of the waltzes Miss Trask had asked breathlessly, 'You are aware of Kenneth's idiosyncrasy?'

'Yes, I am.'

'It doesn't worry you?'

'No, of course not. Why should it? He's a good person,' Betty had said.

'Why should it? It oughtn't to worry anyone – you are quite right, Betty. Should we be daring and attempt this tango?'

They had danced the tango on the end of Morecambe Pier. Betty remembered the opening words of the song, 'Here am I with you, in a world of blue.' Betty shuddered; her bath water had begun to get chilled. She climbed from her world of sea-foam and enchanted remembrances. She clasped the huge bath towel about her and dried her chaste scarred body. She put on her dressing-gown and peered at her face in the mirror. Not a good feature there; small weak eyes, dull grey hair, a sallow complexion, facial hair on the upper-lip and a small wart perched on her left nostril. Betty smiled at her reflection and murmured, 'I'm very fortunate – very fortunate.'

The sea mist engulfing the bathroom had now cleared and Betty was able to see the diving male figure stuck on the wall in all its splendour. She viewed the contours of the body dispassionately. The penis looked disproportionately large. Did they hang down like that? It must be odd having something like that trailing from your body. Apparently they went up and down, too. Now that was a miracle. Betty switched off the light. In all truth, she was not the slightest bit interested in those bits and pieces which caused so much joy and trouble for most people. She decided to wear her purple woollen jersey dress for dinner. Perhaps she might wear the heart-shaped brooch that Miss Trask had given her. Kenneth liked a little decoration.

In another reflection (the wardrobe mirror in Kenneth's bedroom) Kenneth straightened the knot in his tie and viewed his image. He wore a grey Harris tweed sports' jacket, dark-grey flannels, a white shirt and a discreet neck-tie. On his feet were black socks and dark brown, brogue shoes. His hair was quite white; it was cut short and well groomed. He looked like a bank manager in his last year before retirement. Kenneth was pleased with what he saw – he hoped that Betty might put on the yellow beret that he had bought for her over a month ago. She had always excused herself by forgetfulness, she had insisted that she liked it – but had not worn it yet. Kenneth sighed. He adored Betty but he did wish that she would attempt a little more style. Before he left his room he took up what he referred to as his 'Finery', and carefully – almost tenderly – folded them. The mere touch of the fine silky garments caused him intense pleasure. He placed the baby-doll nylon nightdress, the brassiere and the fish-net tights all in a large trunk. This trunk was full of similar sparkling and exotic garments. Kenneth allowed himself just one hour a day for his 'gear-time'. Everyone in the house had accepted it and in his old age he was happier than he had ever been.

He had only been 'caught' in his gear once during the whole of his life. That occasion had caused him shock and horror. He was the last to leave his office and had been working late to finish off a mountain of paperwork that no one else wanted to look at. The building was dark save for his rooms. He was tired and felt that he could safely relax and indulge himself a little.

He was sitting at his desk in black stockings, suspenders and bra when the outside door banged open. A rather uncouth looking man of middle years trundled an enormous vacuum cleaner ahead of him. When he saw Kenneth, he whistled between his teeth.

'I won't split on you,' he had said as he closed the door behind him.

'I'll get changed at once. It's very kind of you.' Kenneth had felt relieved.

'No, stay as you are. Stay like that.' The man had then switched on the hoover and left it standing. He stood before Kenneth and uttered a command not a request. 'Stay as you are.'

'Please, I'd rather get . . .' Kenneth's pleas were useless.

'Just do as you're told or I'll be on the fucking telephone.' The man had unbuttoned his flies and thrust that hard part of himself forward. 'Now get down to it.'

He had seized Kenneth's head and pulled it onto himself. He tore away Kenneth's finery as poor Kenneth provided his relief. Throughout the proceedings the man muttered foul obscenities about women, called them bitches, sluts, slags . . . the tirade went on until he had reached orgasm. The man had left whistling whilst Kenneth vomited.

From this time onward Kenneth had known that many men who purported to like women, actually despised and used them. Kenneth saw this as a fraudulent thing to do – Kenneth would never cheat. If this was a sexual experience, Kenneth had chosen never to repeat it. Now, if Betty would only wear something other than those dreadful flannelette nighties, he might marry her – but Betty did not believe in marriage so there would be no point in asking. He glanced about his room; all was tidy; all was in order. 'I hope that she wears the yellow beret, but I won't mention it again,' he thought as he descended the stairway.

Betty greeted Kenneth at the foot of the stairs.

'I'm ready,' she said. She detected some dismay in Kenneth's expression. 'Are you hungry?' she asked.

'Oh, starving, my dear. Ravenous. Let us step out.'

Kenneth took Betty's arm as they strode along the pavement. He expressed no disappointment that she had chosen to be hatless. Instead, he complimented her on the choice of her perfume. Betty thought this was very odd as she was not wearing any. Perhaps it was the sea-foam still lingering around. As they walked down Queensway, Betty paused to look into different types of eating places. There were many such places. In fact half the world's countries seemed to be reflected in eating. Not a continent seemed unrepresented. Betty began to feel very hungry.

'I didn't telephone a booking for our meal. They know

us so well, I'm sure that they will have a table. You do want to eat at Hetty's Pantry, don't you?' Kenneth asked as Betty peered at a huge piece of meat suspended on a vertical spit in the window of a Turkish restaurant.

'Yes, yes, of course, Kenneth. If you wish.' Betty had stopped to watch an olive-skinned, moustachioed man slice layers of meat off the spit with a huge knife. His right hand wielded the scimitar-like blade whilst his left spun the spit.

'One always knows what one is eating at Hetty's. Plain, simple wholesome food,' said Kenneth.

'Yes, I suppose it is.' Betty could not sound euphoric about Hetty's Pantry. Boiled potatoes and tinned peas did fill a space, but they did not titillate the appetite. The man in the window continued to slash at the meat. 'It's quite barbaric, isn't it?' she asked of Kenneth.

'Hetty's – barbaric?' Kenneth was puzzled.

'No, I mean this meat carving.' Betty pointed towards her swordsman. He smiled at them both from the other side of the window-pane.

'Perhaps you would like a change from Hetty's. Something different – although curry does seem to have an effect upon me. I like the taste – but I am often struck with an unfortunate aftermath the next day.'

'I don't think there are any curries on this menu.' Betty pointed to the hand-written menu stuck on the other side of the window-pane.

'It is very reasonably priced, not that you must feel inhibited about cost tonight, Betty. Why, look – we can take in our own wine and there is no charge for corkage. If you wish to eat here, I can get a bottle of champagne from the off-license.'

'I would very much like to eat here, Kenneth. I have never eaten in a Turkish Restaurant. It could be exotic. The Sultan Ahmet; it does sound exotic, doesn't it? It has a definite Middle-Eastern ring. Imagine! Drinking champagne in Turkey.'

After collecting their champagne Kenneth and Betty settled themselves down for a meal in the Sultan Ahmet. An attractive young woman in jeans and void of make-up took their champagne from them and handed them a menu. Both Betty and Kenneth made a quiet appraisal of their surroundings. Kenneth felt that the place did, indeed, reflect Istanbul. East met West here – but not in the way travel-books extolled this impression. The walls were covered with thinly woven cloth of black and red Islamic design. Two huge, garish pictures completed the decoration. They looked like enormous printed tea-towels and one was placed on either side of the large oblong-shaped room. One picture depicted the Ka'ba – a holy place that looked like an office block in the middle of the desert. The other printed towel showed a stag surveying an imaginary glen. Surely, there wasn't venison on the menu? The round tables were covered with plastic table-cloths that Kenneth had last seen in the late 1950s. He was pleased to see them as they were utilitarian and could be well cleaned after each and every separate diner.

For her part, Betty found the background taped music most pleasing. The songs were in Turkish but they had a plaintive, throaty quality which she found very restful. The cooking smells of charcoal grill and roast also engendered a settled, permanent air to the place. The other diners, too, offered comfort, as the place could accommodate families, men eating with women, men eating with men and women eating with women. No one seemed out of place, and everyone seemed to be familiar with and well-disposed towards their surroundings.

The young girl returned with their champagne and poured some out for her customers.

'Good luck,' she said and smiled as if she meant it. Kenneth and Betty toasted Betty's new future and ordered their meal.

'I like it here, Betty,' said Kenneth, 'It is a real find.'

'Yes, I quite agree. The food looks excellent. It is reasonably priced and the atmosphere of the place is so relaxed. The owners seem to live in an acceptance world. Everyone here, everyone working here, appears to be related. There are brothers, sisters, cousins, wives . . . yes, it is most charming. It is almost like dining in their living room . . .' At this moment a boy child with Down's syndrome came out from the kitchen and marched towards Betty's table. He placed some paper serviettes next to Betty; he smiled and said, 'Thank you.' Then he saluted her and marched back to the kitchen.

'What a charming little boy.' Betty's statement was a truth. The girl placed their food before them and seemed glad of Betty's observation.

'He is my young brother. I love him,' she said simply.

Betty sipped her champagne and bit into her succulent lamb chops.

'You see, Kenneth, they don't treat him differently. He is loved and he survives,' she said.

'I see that you are still an educator,' said Kenneth, 'but I agree with what you say.'

'No, in this case, they are the educators. This family are the educators, Kenneth. What a lesson for us all.'

'Indeed,' said Kenneth, 'I agree with you – and I have never tasted lamb chops so beautifully cooked. I think that we could come here at least once a week. I much prefer it to Hetty's Pantry. I think it is most civilised.'

'So do lots of other people.' Betty glanced about her and saw that the restaurant was almost full.

Throughout the rest of the meal Betty and Kenneth exchanged anecdotes about their respective childhoods. Joys were recalled enthusiastically and deprivations declared flatly with disarming honesty. They made one another laugh and they made one another think; they made comparisons but no judgements. This informal therapy left them happy and satisfied. Kenneth left a generous tip behind as they left. The family shook hands with them and the youngest son waved them goodbye. Kenneth took Betty's arm as they walked along the pavement. A voice shouted after them, 'Excuse me, excuse me.' The young waitress was holding something in her hand. 'I think one of you dropped this.' She placed an article of clothing in Betty's palm.

'I don't remember dropping anything.' Betty examined the clothing. Was it a handkerchief?

'It was near your table.' The girl was insistent. Kenneth began to break into a fit of coughing when Betty held up the garment. It was a garter, the kind of garter that can-can-girl dancers wore over plump thighs. Kenneth continued to cough.

'Ah, yes, it's mine,' said Betty, 'An heirloom from my grandmother. I would have hated to have lost it. There you are, dear. That's for your trouble.' She gave the girl 50p, placed the garter in her handbag and took Kenneth's arm.

'Ahem, ahem, I'm sorry about that, Betty. It was a lapse; out of hours, too! I'm most sorry. It must have slipped off. I'm losing weight, you know. I don't know what I would do without you. I would do anything for you – if you wished to marry . . .'

'Kenneth! One should not marry out of gratitude. One does not have to marry for lasting friendship. You already do more than enough for me. And, I see no harm in you wearing a garter if you want to. No fucking harm at all.'

'Betty!'

'I'm sorry, I know you hate bad language, Kenneth. And I have never used it before – but I suddenly felt the need to use it. Perhaps it is a new freedom, now that I have retired.'

'Oh, Betty, I do hope that you are not going to become coarse.' Kenneth's cough had disappeared. He wondered if coarseness might not, after all, suit Betty.

'I shall become exactly what I want to become. This will not entail hurting anyone. I will cheat no one and I will not cheat myself. What is more, if you want to wear a garter, or two garters, I don't see why you shouldn't wear them whenever you like.'

'You offer such bliss, Betty. Such bliss.'

Bliss – this simple yet elusive feeling enveloped Betty Hooper and Kenneth Trask. Betty's ugliness and Kenneth's incongruity were less than skin deep. A wart on your nose or a garter on your thigh. Take your pick – but if you're blessed with them, there's not much point in hating them; Betty had always found that even the most perverse of her pupils improved if they were cherished a little. Accept and cherish a difference and you disperse the anger or the rancour. Betty had no time for bitterness, no time for rancour. Perhaps this was why Mary Goodheart had always feared her and Miss Trask. True courage never took place on the mad histrionics of the battle-field – as often as not it was within the unlikely frame of a Betty Hooper, recognised by many but declared by few. Miss Hooper will not sit on committees, Miss Hooper will not join opportunist groups, Miss Hooper will not seek the adoration of majority or minority groups, Miss Hooper will be . . .

'Now, that is one of the things I would like to do.' Betty paused and stared at a huge bill-board advertising cigarettes.

'You're not going to start smoking, Betty? Surely you have never been tempted to smoke? Why start now?' Kenneth could not keep the concern from his voice.

'No, of course I'm not going to start smoking. I have never ridden on the back of an animal in all my life. Horses seem so nervous – and I'm not sure that they like being ridden. But a camel is different – don't you think?'

Kenneth looked at the advertisement and wondered how a large picture of a camel could possibly entice someone to smoke.

'They are enigmatic creatures, I do agree.' He could not enter Betty's rapture with regard to the camel.

'Yes, I think that they are timeless – biblical. I will ride a camel – I will; sit on history and be carried forwards and backwards in time,' Betty continued to muse.

'It's getting a little chilly; Easter can be treacherous.' Kenneth led Betty gently away. 'Camels sway from side to side,' he added.

'I will ride one,' said Betty.

Kenneth hoped that Betty was merely being fanciful. He would hate for her to be at risk. But then, Betty was not the kind of person that Bedouins would wish to whisk away. On the other hand, one oughtn't underrate her determination.

Three

Sometimes, during occasional conversations with colleagues with whom he had once worked, Bertrand Motion referred to himself as a middle-aged drop-out. This would often cause minor interest or random amusement but as often as not it would start a conversation on the merits of Sartre or Camus or even Laing. When these intellectual discourses started, Bertrand would listen to his ex-colleagues and would invariably decide that he had 'dropped in' rather than 'dropped out'. He did not experience any regret in having given up social work before it gave him up. He had not entered his vocation flippantly. Bertrand did wish to care. He had done just that for twenty years. He had been paid for this task but the emotional batterings that he received far outweighed the salary that was paid out to him.

On the day that his favourite client – seventy-one year old Mrs Tobler – had received a month's prison sentence for shop-lifting, Bertrand decided that he'd had enough. Mrs Tobler had been released after serving two and a half weeks. She had died exactly twelve days after this event – her death coincided with Bertrand's last working day with the Social Services. Mrs Tobler's fascination with silk scarves had finally allowed the judiciary to strangle the life out of her. Prison had finished her – there had been so little that was pretty to look at there. Bertrand's pleas on her behalf had failed to move the local magistrate who launched forth on protection of property and age-related moral fibre. Mrs Tobler had been interested in silk not fibre and that had been the end of the matter. Bertrand's heart was broken. He could no longer work within these boundaries and sought to mend his heart as well as his jangled nerves.

'My mum weren't a bad person, no she weren't. She were very kind,' Eileen (Mrs Tobler's eldest daughter) had remarked over a ham sandwich and a cup of tea after her mother's desolate funeral and burial were complete. 'Would you like a pickled onion, Mr Motion?' Bertrand had accepted the onion and had nodded agreement with Eileen's observations about her own mother.

'I suppose you'll be relieved now she's off your hands. I know she could be a bit of a trial.' Eileen bit into her sandwich as if to emphasise this fact. 'But then, I suppose you have lots of other cases to take her place.'

'Oh yes, I think disturbance of a mental or emotional nature is nurtured in this country.' Bertrand was immediately sorry that he had spoken cynically.

'Pardon?' Fortunately, Eileen had not understood him.

'As a matter of fact, Eileen, I am leaving my job tomorrow.'

'Oh, are you going up the ladder? I am pleased for you. You've been lovely to my mum. I am glad. There's lots of people that will miss you – I dare say.'

'No Eileen, I'm not going up the ladder or down it. I'm getting off it before I fall off it. I'm leaving social work.'

'Oh, Lord, what will you do? You're not young, are you?' Eileen had sounded genuinely concerned.

'I'll do little jobs or jobs for short periods of time. I'll work in a bookshop, perhaps, or a pub, or in a park, or a garden . . .

Eileen had looked astonished at Bertrand and had smiled and nodded. 'He's going down the drain,' she had thought. 'Good luck,' she murmured, but shook her head as he left. Her response was exactly the same as that of Bertrand's social work team leader. One didn't need a qualification to recognise a failure.

Now, two years later, Bertrand did not feel like a failure. He sat in the kitchen at 11 a.m. awaiting Betty who had left to put on her coat. They always shopped together on Saturday mornings. Since leaving his job, Bertrand (always of a romantic nature) had tended to fall in love quite frequently. Men drifted comfortably into Bertrand's bed but left it rather quickly on account of his enthusiasm for sudden and complete commitment. After every fuck, Bertrand was convinced he was in love. He was ready to believe the mysterious mutterings of men within the environment of the orgasm. He had not realised that the kind of love he required was more likely to be declared in the midst of domesticity rather than passion. Receiving a bit of semen (one way or another) was hardly a passport to deep, trusting love. The semen that found its way into or onto Bertrand dried up and cemented nothing. He tried too hard.

'I hope I didn't wake you up this morning, Betty,' Bertrand spoke as Betty came in. 'You are wise to wear a scarf, it's a bit chilly out. I was up at 6 a.m. – I walked with Ashok to the tube station. You know, Betty, I think that this is the real thing this time.'

'Oh, I'm glad,' said Betty. This was the third 'real thing' in a year and Bertrand had now slept with Ashok twice. 'Where did you meet him?'

'At work. He is one of the dubbing assistants. We finish this film in three weeks and I start on another one the week after completion. Of course, I'll still keep in touch with Ashok. I hope to go to India next year – enter the culture or let it seep into me.'

Betty assumed that had already happened. 'It's a very varied culture,' she said.

'Yes, isn't it, and what contradictions of cruelty and

tenderness it expresses,' Bertrand sighed. More in desperation than vocation he had begun to do 'voice-overs' for various products on commercial radio. His dulcet tones could bend and glide and add various shades of meaning to a new mindless musical or a double-glazed bathroom. The dubbing of Indian films had proved a new source of employment. He sounded much more convincing in unlikely situations than many more professionally trained performers. It was not difficult for Bertrand to enter the spirit of life and death romance at the bleep of a button.

'Now you have seen the situation – the lovers have been sentenced to death for adultery. They are to die together; they are allowed one minute together. The camera fade-out with the large doors closing on them allows some imagination on your part. He is of high birth; she is a slave girl. They have sacrificed their lives for this one minute of love. All we show is the great heavily studded door. We wait the sounds of love-making built up to a climax, his and hers. I will count to sixty – time your responses to that.' The director was surprised at the skill and alacrity with which both Bertrand and his actress partner had applied themselves to the task. 'One' – 'mm–' – 'two' – 'mm–mm' – 'three' – 'oh, oh' – 'four' – 'ah–ah–ah . . .'

Bertrand had closed his eyes and thought of Ashok; sighs, groans and quiet endearments spilled forth. As the director shouted 'cut' to the dubbing controller, Bertrand had continued to moan and was embarrassed to find that he had eventually covered the entire head of the microphone with his mouth. The shape of it was not unattractive but the texture was not to his liking. That night, Ashok had gone home with him and Bertrand had entered a sexual fantasy relationship with his partner that was not too far removed from sixth century India.

Although she was ready to leave, Betty sat down opposite Bertrand and viewed him from the other side of the kitchen table. She knew that Bertrand wanted to talk, and she knew that if she did not listen to his euphoria their shopping expedition would be ruined. Bertrand was often forgetful at such times. During his last 'real thing' he had bought a three-foot live eel for Sunday lunch – stating that it would make a change from a chicken or a joint. That particular Sunday lunch had been an abject failure. On seeing the eel swishing and swimming happily in the sink Kenneth had fainted. Betty had flatly declared that she could not cook it – let alone kill it; and Bertrand himself had finally taken the creature in a bucket of water and tipped it into the canal. All this was on account of an Icelandic trawler owner who had caught Bertrand in his net whilst holidaying in London. Betty sat and waited whilst Bertrand lit a cigarette. He took two long drags and issued forth.

'Ashok is telephoning me at three this afternoon just to hear my voice. It is dreadful for both of us being separated for even that amount of time.' Betty glanced at her watch as Bertrand delivered this information. It was now 11.30 a.m. 'I wonder if you would mind just reading through this script. It's the final scene – we do the complete dubbing on Monday.' Bertrand handed Betty the script. 'Could you read the slave girl's part, Betty? I don't expect you to put any expression into it. Just give me the cues.'

'Heartbeats.' Betty read the first line.

'No, dear, no, not that. That is the title of song that is being sung before we start – when the song fades out, we come in. It's the next line that is yours.'

'Ah, my love, my life.' Betty did her best – but she did not sound like a slave girl.

'I hold you in my arms and I encompass the universe. Your breasts are nature's pillows. It is there I lay my head.'

'Oh, oh, ah, ah,' Betty crooned flatly.

'I am bounden to you. Bonded. I wish for no release.'

'Who is supposed to be the slave? The girl or the man?' Betty asked.

'Please, please don't butt in on the script, Betty. They are slaves to their mutual passion. Don't forget they are dying for it.' Bertrand could not keep a trace of pique from his voice and Betty decided not to question the script's credibility. She had all the vegetables and meat to purchase for the weekend and the dry cleaners closed at 2 p.m.

'Take me, do your will, my will, upon me.'

'I remove your gown. I feast my eyes on your body. I touch your shoulders with my finger-tips. I caress your neck and your breasts with my mouth . . .'

'Oh,' said Betty.

'That "Oh", Betty, is a sign of pleasure. Don't say it as though you have just dropped a cup and saucer.' Bertrand coughed slightly after this gentle reprimand and continued:

'Your body is the world – I explore it. All its secret, unknown places – the mountains, the terrain, the sweet-scented estuary. I swim in it. I plunge deep and with all my being . . .'

'Oh, oh, oh, fade out.'

'No, Betty, not "Fade out". That's just a recording direction. After that we consummate.' Bertrand relieved Betty of her script; she would never make an actress, he thought.

'Good Lord – do they consummate on the screen?'

'Oh, no, there is just faint background music and we make love sounds for one minute. There are shots of wild horses running through a canyon and flamingos taking flight from the water whilst that takes place. After that we are both taken for execution in the market place.' Bertrand shook his head sadly.

'Our market will be crowded if we don't leave soon and the best of the spring greens will be gone.' Betty thought it better to centre Bertrand's thoughts on the present and the living rather than the past and the dead. She thought it odd that historical appeal should so often give or tinge barbarism with romance. Once on a visit to a museum in South Kensington she had noticed a great crowd of people standing around an altar-piece. She was initially pleased that something devotional could attract so much attention. She could still hear the thin correct voice of the lady with plastic covers over her shoes as she cooed over the deaths of different saints which decorated the piece. 'Ah, that one is being sawn in half. Oh, she is being boiled in oil. They are tearing that one with hooks. I'm not quite sure about him. He is upside down and they are burning the . . .' Betty shuddered at the thought of the altar-piece and the crowd that savoured it.

'You're not cold are you, Betty?'

'No, someone was walking over my grave – or the graves of saints. I am ready. Shall we go? I do believe a bit of sunshine has broken through the cloud.' Betty peered from the window and was glad to see chimney pots without smoke, a city without fire or sword, a city where shopping for vegetables could be a pleasure. Betty was glad of the present and sought to remind Bertrand that he was part of it by handing him two shopping bags.

Four

As Betty and Bertrand wended their way through the vegetable barrows of the Portobello Road, Kenneth Trask was putting forth a noble offer of service in order that a large group of people should not have their enthusiastic and artistic aspirations destroyed by an unexpected assailant. The assailant was diarrhoea and it had assaulted one of the actresses taking part in the Peak Scene Players' matinee production of Dylan Thomas's *Under Milk Wood*.

The Peak Scene Players were a group of twenty-four people who had chosen to explore their artistic potential through the medium of dramatic art. All of them were involved in the mundane pressures of office or professional work during the day but on two evenings of each week they trod the magic of the boards. These evenings fed their yearning hearts whilst the days fed their rumbling stomachs.

Under Milk Wood had seemed an odd choice. None of the company was Welsh – only three had ever been to Wales and the parochial ironies and flavour of the piece did not impress anyone too much. Also, this particular piece was being done at a local sixth form college, a local church drama group and by a London Transport Amateur Dramatic Company. However, as each member had a part and as each could account for ten friends or relatives attending a performance, then a captive audience was assured.

Now, half an hour before the curtain was due to rise the company were distraught. There were sixty-five parts in the play – each member was already duplicated and in some cases triplicated. There was not a woman to spare who could possibly play Mrs Dai Bread One, Dulcie Prothero and Lil the Gluepot. It was left to Kenneth to put forward a 'show must go on' offer – whatever the sacrifice.

'It won't be necessary for our stage-manager to read out these parts.' There was a murmur of dissent amongst some members of the company as they could see little alternative to this emergency ploy. Some of them were in various stages of undress and the cramped dressing space was causing minor squabbles as shoes, stockings and various other garments tended to get mislaid. The director of the piece felt that a degree of tension before a performance was not necessarily a bad thing, but this sudden indisposition had created an atmosphere that verged on panic. Kenneth held up his hand as though he were an evangelical Welsh preacher.

'I first heard this play on the radio many years ago. I have a tape-recording of it and have often listened to it. It may come as a surprise to you, but I can assure you that I know all the parts. In fact, I can recite the whole piece in its entirety.'

'People have not come here tonight to listen to a recitation, they have come to see a production,' the director snapped irritably.

'Ah, I wouldn't dream of offering to recite the whole piece.' Kenneth was not being strictly honest on this point. He continued, 'No, with the help of a little female attire, a little make-up, head-scarves and woollen hats –' he paused for dramatic effect – 'I can play Mrs Dai Bread One, Dulcie Prothero, and Lil the Gluepot.' All murmurings faded. The company fell silent. The boldness of the suggestion had shocked them into acquiescence but no one seemed to want to second it. Finally, it was the voice of authority which lent its support to Kenneth's offer.

Linden-Parry had sat as a High Court judge for many years. In that capacity he had often made pronouncements which were listened to – and accepted – when he was well past his dotage. He had been quite capable of delivering a silly homily and make it sound like an innate truth. His foggy Welsh background had given him the skills of an orator or an actor. He was known to be a 'character' and his 'presence' was always admired. In his retirement he accepted leading roles with the Peak Scene Players. His portrayal of Captain Cat was full of authority.

'Splendid! Splendid! A capital idea,' he boomed. 'Let us not waste another minute. Kenneth is to be congratulated on his public-spiritedness. Let us all prepare for the matinee performance without more ado.' At this point the director concurred and the players turned their attention to themselves and the characters they were to play. The sounds of taped Welsh choir-music drifted from the auditorium and a church hall in Bayswater became a chapel in Wales.

During earlier rehearsals of the play the director had insisted that the play should be delivered in its entirety without an interval in order to maintain language flow and continuity. After complaints from some older members of the cast this approach had to be modified, as some of the older players were suffering from shortage of breath as entrances, exits, and quick changes of dress took their physical toll. The director had finally ceded to a short interval of eight minutes in order to allow some of his gasping performers time to rest. The curtain had been drawn for this intermission and relatives and friends applauded generously; they had all recognised someone that they knew on stage and felt well satisfied.

'Good Lord, I don't know how you manage it, Kenneth. I hadn't imagined you would have had time to look so authentic underneath as well as on top. It is quite amazing,' observed a young man behind stage to Kenneth. Kenneth thought that the man looked Welsh or Celtic, as he was dark-haired and pale-skinned. Apart from a jock-strap, his only clothing were thatches of black hair that adorned his chest, his wrists, his pubic regions and even his shoulders. Takis Angelides was, in fact, a Londoner of Greek origin. Perhaps it was his Mediterranean roots that had been stirred by Kenneth's present exotic appearance. The jock-strap appeared to be troubling him. 'I find that gear a bit of a turn-on,' he added.

Kenneth quickly seized his third costume and began pulling it over his shoulders. He certainly did not want to flaunt his brassiere, suspender-belt, frilly knickers, black stockings to all and sundry. Although, from an artistic point of view they had helped him to 'enter' his roles.

'Capital, Kenneth. I must say you were capital,' Matthew Linden-Parry congratulated Kenneth as he turned from viewing him through the wash-basin mirror. This remark was answered by a snapping sound as Kenneth swivelled one of his suspenders into position beneath his dress. 'Ah, just sorting your new geography about, eh? How about coming to my place for tiffing after the show?'

'That would be most pleasant; thank you,' Kenneth replied, as he adjusted his headscarf.

'My driver is calling to collect me. See you later – must pay nature a call before second curtain.' Matthew patted Kenneth on the shoulder as he left.

'What's tiffing?' asked Takis. 'I thought that I knew all the kinks – I've tried everything. Can I come?'

'Tiffing is having a drink, Takis. Usually a gin and tonic – I think that the military in India used the expression. I think that you ought to get dressed.' Kenneth glanced down at Takis' hips. 'Yes, do get dressed, Takis – you are on stage in three minutes and I do not think that you are supposed to be carrying a spear.'

Some ninety-five minutes after this exchange Kenneth and Matthew Linden-Parry were settling themselves down in Linden-Parry's large South Kensington mansion flat. As Kenneth sank into the great leather armchair, he felt that he was a long way from a Welsh village. The room was imbued with conservative intellect and aestheticism. The paintings adorning the walls were largely dull but valuable water-colours: seascape or landscape, one could take one's pick. A dark maroon and black Indian carpet covered most of the floor, whilst objets d'art took the form of three Chinese vases, and the large bookcase held no novels more daring than Mrs Gaskell and Emily Bronte. The high windows were heavily curtained in deep blue velvet and cream net. A clock chimed far too often.

'Ah, I'll get you a drink. My housekeeper comes between 7 a.m. and 1 p.m. – and then again from 8 p.m. to 10 p.m. Just to answer domestic needs, you understand.' Here, Matthew paused to chuckle, or was it titter? 'I have never chosen to take a lady wife. By the time I thought I would need it, the investment wasn't necessary. Ah, your drink. I'm forgetting. I'll just put on a little music – so soothing and restful, I always find.' Matthew pressed a tape-button concealed behind a cabinet with shortened ivory tusks as legs; then left Kenneth alone.

Kenneth leaned back in the armchair and closed his eyes – he did feel a little tired now. A natural reaction after the afternoon's elation. 'I hope he will not bring a large gin and tonic. I handle alcohol so badly,' he thought. 'I suppose he's put on some Sibelius or perhaps Beethoven. Yes, Beethoven would fit in with the place.' Suddenly Kenneth sat bolt upright. The music had begun – and it was not Beethoven. Kenneth was most perplexed by what he was hearing and supposed that Matthew had inadvertently chosen the wrong tape.

Some American singer of the Forties or even Thirties was singing an odd song entitled 'They Wear Them

Higher in Hawaii'. The singer sang this as 'They Wear Them Hiya in Hawaya'. Kenneth allowed for poetic licence but still found the song a little vulgar. It was not the kind of song that he would have expected Matthew Linden-Parry to be remotely interested in. There must be some kind of mistake.

'Oh!' The exclamation came from Kenneth as Matthew entered carrying two small glasses of sherry (just larger than thimble size) on a tiny tray.

'Hope you like sherry. It's dry. Sherry has to be dry.' Matthew offered the tray to Kenneth who took one of the glasses. Kenneth gulped and puked. He felt unable to speak. It was not the music, nor the meanness of the drink offered that had taken away his speech, but Matthew's appearance.

'Nice ditty, isn't it?' Matthew smilingly referred to the music and twirled around. For someone of such comfortable rotundity Matthew was most agile. He managed to get in two side-kicks and a double twirl as the last bars of the song ended.

'It's a dinky little song, isn't it?' Matthew enquired again.

Kenneth could still only manage to nod and break into a watery unenthusiastic smile of assent. This was encouragement enough for Matthew.

'Here is my favourite – came out sometime after that one – it never fails to revive me. Sets me all of a tingle.' He clicked on another tape.

Kenneth, now transfixed to his chair, watched Matthew Linden-Parry – resplendent in a black corset, silver-spangle stockings and high-heeled shoes – perform a South Seas courtship dance to the music of a song entitled 'She Wears Red Feathers and A Huli-Huli Skirt'. Kenneth was relieved that at the end of the record Matthew was having problems with his breathing. Whether this was due to an excess of dancing or the tightness of the corset he could not decide. His relief was so great that he knocked back the other sherry.

'Ah, I thought that I had poured both glasses?' Matthew looked puzzled at the two empty glasses as he sank into the other chair opposite Kenneth.

'You did. I'm sorry, I drank them both. Er – I wasn't thinking what I was doing.' Kenneth's truthfulness often caused him to suffer where others would not.

This short moment of truth proved no exception. Matthew leapt from his chair, left the room and returned in a large dark brown dressing-gown with the monogram of some army coat-of-arms on its pocket. Something in Latin encircled the motif.

Matthew's voice and manner had changed. He warned Kenneth of the inherent dangers of alcohol and then told him that he was soon due at his club. Kenneth's dismissal was as abrupt as his invitation. Justice did not come into it – justice was a game. Kenneth was not prepared to leave this particular dock in an undignified manner.

'Perhaps you would order me a cab – I feel a little dizzy.'

'Ah, you see – the sherry.' Matthew spoke with great justification.

'No, no, it was the pirouettes. If they are badly exercised they can throw an onlooker off balance.'

From the cab window Kenneth stared intently at buildings and persons that dotted the city. The enormous political slogan on a large bill-board was a blatant lie.

Could eleven men in shirts and shorts kicking a ball around a field really cause thousands of other men to jeer, cheer and dole out gratuitous violence to other people that they did not know?

What an enormous number of police there seemed to be nowadays. Could the job be vocational for all of them? Bingo-halls must be safe places; there were so many of them. All these long queues of plain middle-aged men and women – were all their enthusiasms reduced?

As the cab paused at the red light on the traffic signal, the driver turned and spoke to Kenneth through the window aperture.

'They've lost again, yer know. One–nil.'

'I'm sorry,' said Kenneth. Again, this was the truth as Kenneth thought that loss was similar to bereavement. One was never quite the same again – but then, the change might be an improvement. He paid his fare and felt happy to be home again – in a curious way there was some satisfaction in being in many ways alien to a culture of which he was part. There was even some comfort in adversity.

Instead of going straight into the flat, he called in to help out at the launderette. Someone had overloaded a machine and the floor was flooded with soapy water. It was fun paddling around with a mop. People were laughing and smiling. Bubbles floated through the air. They burst here and there when they were ready.

Five

Bertrand was unable to accept any comfort from either Betty or Kenneth. The telephone had not rung and Bertrand's whole life now seemed to depend on his new lover Ashok – as though this man were some kind of life-support machine. Bertrand sat at the kitchen table, his head resting on his arms. He had asked Betty to check the telephone in case it was out of order. She had done this and reported that it was working perfectly. Bertrand had sighed and murmured – hopeless – hopeless; he had accepted a cup of tea from Kenneth but it had gone cold without his lips touching it. A faint skin, like the algae on stagnant ponds, now floated on the top of it.

'I'll pour you another cup. It's still fresh,' said Kenneth.

'No, don't, thank you. I'm not thirsty.' Bertrand would not be comforted.

From past experience, Betty had learned that in these situations it was better not to offer Bertrand consolation. There had been six of these great loves since Bertrand had stayed with her, and each and every one of them had broken Bertrand's heart. Betty had observed that his heart always managed to mend itself after each breakage. Romantic hearts always had this capacity – perhaps that is why so many of them seemed to cling on for so long.

Bertrand had been grief-stricken when Errol, his West Indian friend, had left him to go off with a Methodist minister. He had remained silent for nearly a week when his friend Gary, a motorbike enthusiast, had merely sent him a note thanking him for the new crash helmet and the studded leather jacket and explaining how he couldn't see him any more on account of a controlled relationship that he had now entered. Bertrand had been traumatised by this – but had recovered. Now Ashok his Indian friend had not telephoned. Bertrand raised his head and Kenneth and Betty waited expectantly for the sad, profound utterance.

'*C'est tout fini*. It's all over.' He shook his head from side to side. 'As far as I am concerned the world might just as well end today.'

'Oh, dear!' Betty murmured.

Her murmurings were not on account of Bertrand's gloomy outlook but referred to the crockery on the kitchen table and the china ornaments that adorned the mantelpiece.

'Dear God in Heaven!' Kenneth cried out, not in blasphemy but in need.

Even Bertrand's present state of melancholic torpor was broken as the cups and saucers and ornaments began to rattle. Earth tremors were a new experience to all of them and they remained attentive but immobile as the rattling increased. When the teapot overturned and the milk bottle spilled its contents over the floor Kenneth cried out again.

'Poltergeists. Stand still.'

This command was promptly disobeyed as the light bulb plus its glass shade came adrift and crashed onto the table top. Without direction Betty, Bertrand and Kenneth all found themselves in kneeling positions underneath the table. In cases of emergency all three were used to recognising real shelter for one reason or another.

'It's like war-time air-raids.' Betty spoke into Bertrand's bottom which was positioned a few inches from her nose. Space was not a luxury they could afford in this present situation. Ever practical, Betty added, 'It can't be atomic or we would be blistering by now.' The room continued to shake as falling debris and plaster rained over their household.

'Listen! Is that a siren?' Kenneth asked.

A high-pitched whining and whirring noise hummed through the room as though several swarms of bees had simultaneously been released. It grew louder and more insistent to the point where it seemed the sound barrier might well be broken. There was a cracking sound and then great gurgling and grinding noises – and all was still. The fugitives remained where they were. Intrepid explorers often met their doom by venturing too far too soon. Betty, Bertrand and Kenneth waited; impatience might prove more lethal than discomfort.

The dreadful convulsion that had seized their kitchen had now ceased; milk dripped from the table and trickled to the ground, forming a white estuary which meandered along the kitchen floor near Betty. She could hear the drops dripping from their source and feeding the flood below. Another noise broke this pattern of events. Betty raised her finger. Her body language conveyed the question to Bertrand and Kenneth. They nodded. Yes, they could both hear the tapping. Did this now herald some fresh onslaught? The tapping continued.

It was Betty who ventured forth first; crawling on all fours she made her way from underneath the table towards the kitchen window which looked out onto the main street. She looked up and saw the head and shoulders of a ginger-haired man in his late twenties. She saw him tap at the window. He did not look alien or aggressive; indeed, there was an expression of real concern upon his pale face. Perhaps it was this distress that caused his acne to look so omnipresent.

Betty rose to her feet and watched the man's face break into a relieved smile. His mime indicated that he wished her to open the window. Betty motioned Kenneth and Bertrand to join her. Kenneth opened the window. Were they going to rescue this man or had he come to rescue them?

'I'm sorry. Is everybody OK? Oh, I do hope so. I'm the new manager of the launderette below.' He smiled again. 'You might say I've had a baptism of fire.' He gripped the sides of the ladder with both hands. 'Yes, a baptism of fire.'

'I wonder if you might explain yourself a little more fully.' Kenneth felt the need of a little formality. The day had been far too eventful for him and it was not yet over. Survivors ought never to feel too grateful. There was always another hurdle, another precipice, another river to cross . . .

'You see we installed the new bumper washing-machine – it washes a hundredweight of linen at one go. Useful for some of the hotels around here. They need to change their sheets three or four times a day, sometimes more than that. Other peoples' stains aren't very appealing are they?' The ginger man extended his palm as though he were awaiting some change. 'Oh dear, it's begun to rain.'

'You had better come inside,' said Betty. Bertrand helped the man through the open window space into the kitchen. Betty indicated that they should all sit. This they did, although their surroundings now indicated that they had sat through a bomb blast and ignored it. 'You were saying?' Betty was interested to hear the rest of the narrative.

'Well, the machine has been busy all day – you would expect that, wouldn't you? Friday nights and Saturdays are always energetic. Yes, we had loaded the machine for the umpteenth time – and when it reached its spin cycle it just seemed to say, enough is enough.' The man began to gather bits of broken china from the table and heap them into a plastic bowl. He continued as the fragments were dropped into the bowl piece by piece.

'It just took off, the bloody machine took off. Jumped

from its platform and careered around the place like a bloody armoured tank. We are flooded out down there. I suppose we took it past its limit. Now we have paid for it.'

'So, it seems – have we,' said Kenneth glancing about him.

'Ah, don't worry. You can claim all expenses and more. The machine is fully insured. The firm will pay out well. This is not the kind of publicity they want for a new product. They want to sell it abroad. Export, you know.'

'Oh, I'm sure the Russians and Americans will be more than interested,' said Kenneth. 'They might want to drop it somewhere.'

'Just send the bill to me – make it out generous to yourselves, you deserve compensation. Here is my card.' The man gave Betty his card, apologised once more and waved goodbye as he disappeared down the ladder.

'Well, I don't suppose we will ever have an experience like that again,' said Kenneth.

'It would be impossible to repeat,' Bertrand observed.

'I experienced something like it before.' Betty spoke sadly.

'Really?'

'Oh, Betty, honest?'

This chorus was now curious. Betty was back in her story telling corner. She was now only a lay-teacher, but her skill had not waned.

'It was during the war. I was in what would now be termed as a sixth-form, studying for something called a Higher School Certificate. I attended an endowed Girls' Grammar School in the city some miles away from my home. I was a P.G.T. There were only about twenty of us in the whole school.'

'A P.G.T. – were you proscribed in some way?' Kenneth interrupted gently. He never enjoyed stories with too much mystery and had never been interested in denouement.

'Poor Girl's Trust – yes, I passed an examination that gave me a half-passport to privilege. P.G.T. girls attended that school as though they were being done a permanent favour. You see, our school fees were paid for by a charity. The parents of the other girls bought their tickets. Even so, we P.G.T's could barely afford our uniforms and endless sports accessories for games like hockey and lacrosse.

'A mistress of general demeanour inspected us each and every day. Our navy blue skirts had to be the correct length. No dipping hem-lines; blouses had to be, oh, so white and uncrumpled. Blazers without stain and shining brass buttons. Oh, yes, uniform exterior was most important. Worst of all were the wretched hats with wide brims. They were a most expensive item.

'Many of us had bought our hats second-hand and we had to try to attempt to preserve them as though they were some kind of religious relic. Most of the teachers were kind to us – but the mistress of general demeanour was even an exception to their patronising charity. In short, she was a civilised, cruel bitch.

'Eileen Cresswell was the grubbiest of us all. She was made to feel the deprivation of her family. It made no difference to this foul teacher that Eileen's mother had been widowed in the first year of the war. It made no difference that Eileen had to look after two younger brothers and a younger sister. Her mother worked "nights" in a munitions factory. Mrs Gladthorne, our mistress of demeanour and teacher of Divinity and Latin, bullied her every day.

' "Eileen, do try giving your hair another two minutes brushing, dear – morning *and* evening. It will take that tangled look out of it. Use a good quality brush, mind – if the beginnings are good the rest will follow."

'Mrs Gladthorne never forgave our "beginnings". As far as she was concerned we were dandruff that should not be there.

'Some of the girls would toady and fawn about her – as is often the case with the victims of bullies. Poor Eileen would remain silent, injured too deeply to express any emotion. Her withdrawn and morose behaviour only seemed to spur Mrs Gladthorne on to greater heights.

'"Eileen, my dear, what are we going to do about your hat?" Here she tittered and cordially invited some of the more wickedly obedient girls to join her. "Sh, sh, sh, girls. Now do not be unkind." She had raised her forefinger in feigned disapproval. "We can't have you coming to school like a female version of Hop-a-long Cassidy or Tom Mix, can we?" There were more suppressed giggles and titters, and I remember Eileen's white and expressionless face. She took off her hat and placed it in her lap. She held it most gently, almost as if – almost as if it were a newborn baby.

'"No, dear, for your own esteem, I suggest that you steam it. It might bring a little more shape back into it, although perhaps I am being too hopeful. Even the most treasured garments have to be laid to rest sometimes." Eileen had nodded and said nothing, but kept stroking the hat with the utmost tenderness.' Betty stroked her nose reflectively and continued.

'We never lost our sense of decorum – it was just not allowed – not even during air-raids. On this particular day we were all assembled ready to depart for home. It was November and wet and cold and although it was only just after 4 p.m. it was almost dark. The P.G.T. girls always made their way through the shopping areas towards the bus-stop in single file. It was called a crocodile. But unlike crocodiles we could not eat in transit. Fish and chips were never allowed. Nor could we speak to one another or answer calls from boys and girls attending the Secondary Modern Schools. We were an enforced tragic elite. We had just lined up when the sirens began to wail.

'With a minimum of fuss we moved across the playground and climbed over an old stone wall which bordered a decrepit churchyard. Here, we all entered an enormous vault – built for some family's joint burial a hundred years before. The place was now a resting place for the living and the dead.

'We could hear the aeroplanes and then a series of dull thudding noises. We were frightened but none of us called out. And then, Eileen Cresswell seemed to gasp with horror as though she had witnessed something vile and terrible. She clasped her hand to her mouth. And then . . . and then she ran from us all – up the steps of the vault and out into the danger-fraught, dark afternoon.'

'Oh dear. Had she become panic-stricken?' asked Kenneth.

'Poor girl . . . poor child,' Bertrand murmered.

'No, she wasn't a victim of panic but a victim of education,' said Betty. Her tone had now become cold and shaken. 'She was killed by bomb-blast. Her shattered body was found near to our classroom. In her right hand she clutched her hat. She had forgotten it, you see – and had gone to rescue it. Gone to rescue that fucking hat on behalf of Mrs Gladthorne and all that ta-ra-ra. When we emerged from the vault there was rubble and chaos everywhere and in the midst of it all, there was Eileen.'

Kenneth, Bertrand and Betty all began to methodically straighten up the kitchen at this point in the story. They worked swiftly not speaking much and within an hour it was all in order.

'You know, after her death, the school treated Eileen as though she were a martyr. She was revered and talked of with pride. It was at about this time that I decided to become a teacher – if only I could manage to get rid of some of the gruesome conformity and barbarism that Gladthorne and others like her had perpetrated, then I would have achieved something. A small ambition.' Betty smiled sadly, and paused as if she were about to announce a quiet benediction – and then the telephone began to ring.

Six

'Oh, Ashok, I thought you were never going to call.' Bertrand could not keep the tinge of relief from his voice as he spoke into the mouth-piece of the telephone, 'It's 8 p.m. – I have been waiting all afternoon. I've been so worried, imagining all sorts of terrible things that might have happened to you.'

'Terrible? Terrible? What terrible thing could happen to me in an afternoon? I have been sleeping.' Ashok's response was curt and sharp.

'I'm sorry. It was silly of me,' Bertrand answered contritely, although he had nothing to be contrite about. 'I have missed you. When are we going to meet again?' Unconsciously, Bertrand's conversation with Ashok was not too far away from his voice-overs for the Indian epic.

'You will see me at work – next Thursday, I think. It is the final run-through. You will see me then,' Ashok all but snapped back. 'I wonder if you could just run through the garden scene now. I wish to edit it and I haven't a hope here, at home.'

Bertrand thought that this request was very odd but said: 'Of course, of course. Just wait. I'll get the script.' He returned and picked up the telephone. He could hear Ashok breathing. Had Ashok ever suffered from asthma? 'Are you there?'

'Yes, yes, go on, go on.' Ashok sounded urgent. 'Please begin where she removes her robe from his shoulders. I will cough when you should begin . . . Ahem.'

Bertrand had some slight qualms concerning Ashok's telephone bill but began. It was a long extract, just over fifteen minutes in length and it seemed to possess less poetry without the usual sitar accompaniment. Nevertheless, his dulcet tones began to bend and glide around the text, providing varied shades of meaning and ambiguity to prose which was dull and romantic. Interpretation from Bertrand was always original.

For some reason the high-born Indian prince had been strapped to a tree in his own gardens. This was some form of atonement or penance inflicted on him by his parents for daring to show something akin to affection for one of the Palace's slave girls.

On screen the slaves saw the tree with the unfortunate prince's arms pinioned around it. His frontage was obscured by the tree trunk and suitable foliage.

The slave girl had heard news of his distress and had boldly sought him in the garden to offer what comfort she could. Again, the viewer could see little of her but trails of silk sari which fluttered from either side of the tree and foliage like butterfly wings.

The wings fluttered up and down the hidden torso as though in search of some strange nectar. These delicate caresses and hoverings seemed to give the prince the most agonised pleasure and appeared to leave him exhausted but content. Bertrand delivered his last anguished cry, 'I am spilled. I am lost.'

A strange gasping sound came from the earpiece – followed by a long sigh.

'Hello, hello Ashok. Are you there? Are you alright?' Bertrand could hear breathing, but there was no reply.

'Ashok, are you there?'

'Yes, of course I am.'

'Oh, when am I going to see you?' Bertrand hovered about the mouthpiece.

'I hope never.'

Bertrand was swatted away by these three words, his gossamer wings torn from him. He felt too broken for reply.

'Your image does not match your voice – or my image of your voice. I have no need to see you.' The receiver made a clicking noise and Bertrand was transported from sitars and a jasmine scented garden to a burring tone and an empty hallway. He banged the receiver down and let out a single strangled cry of rage and stormed into the kitchen.

'I'm a bloody idiot, a stupid fool,' he shouted as he entered. His self-denigratory observations (which were not wholly true) were delivered to an empty room. Betty and Kenneth had fled to their own rooms. As is often the case with close friends, they knew that the telephone call was to be an emotional demolition. Sexual intercourse was often riddled with duplicity by one partner or another, or even by both. It was a pastime Betty had never been tempted to indulge in. Kenneth was much too honest to deceive, so that his encounters had been rare and not missed.

Bertrand took up four tabloid newspapers and sat himself at the table. It was his habit to buy at least three of these papers every day. All of these papers purported to represent the average and ordinary reader. Yet, many of them seemed to be appalled when the ordinary person seemed to be extraordinary. Good news about the ordinary person did not seem to be the order of the day – tragic or wounding news was recorded faithfully, some-times even imaginatively. Bertrand read the agony aunts (who were truthful) and studied the competitions.

Most of the competitions did not really require study, but they required ticks. Like some bored school-teacher approaching essays on *Jane Eyre* for the five hundredth time, Bertrand sprayed ticks against various letters.

Sometimes he crossed out a sentence; sometimes he underlined one. Then he wrote his address at the bottom of the competition slip. He had experienced a limited success up to this time. He had won a vacuum-cleaner, a pedigree pony (which he had been forced to give away to a charity) and a set of electrified hair-curlers. He had never expected to win – but this mild form of gambling gave him some kind of slender hope in the future when he was feeling a little low.

It was now 10.30 p.m. Kenneth called from his room: 'Time for your cocoa, Betty. I'll just put the milk on. It will be ready in five minutes.'

Kenneth was pleased to see Bertrand placing his competition entries in envelopes. This usually signified that Bertrand was intent on recovering from a lost love. His decline over this most recent one was obviously not going to be too prolonged.

'Would you like a cup of cocoa, Bertrand?' Kenneth did not want to sound too sympathetic and he asked his question without turning from the gas-stove.

'How kind. Yes, I would like a cup of cocoa. I'm not going out tonight. I feel the need to be domestic.' Bertrand licked his first-class stamps and stuck them on the envelopes. 'Stamp designs have improved over the years, haven't they?'

Kenneth 'mm-mm-ed' assent to this question but was quietly hoping that Bertrand would in the future continue to 'feel the need to be domestic.' The cleaning of the house was left to Betty and Kenneth.

'I can't think why you are both concerned with externals.' Bertrand had remarked on numerous occasions when Kenneth might have been cleaning the kitchen floor or Betty vacuuming the stairs.

One could always tell when Bertrand had bathed, as he left his own plimsoll line in the bath behind him. Neither Betty or Kenneth had ever entered Bertrand's room – but neither had ever been aware of him cleaning it. If he was expecting a guest Bertrand tended to use a strongly scented aerosol spray. A very heavy smell of hyacinths had pervaded the stairway for the last fortnight because of this.

Domestic costs did not affect Bertrand's pocket. Household goods were purchased by Betty and Kenneth. Washing-up liquid, toilet-paper, soap – all were necessities which Bertrand sought not to recognise. Nevertheless, he did use them; unromantic objects were often the foundation for romance. Bertrand did not invest sufficiently in such commonplace foundations. Kenneth had come to believe that Bertrand needed to be continually disappointed and grieved as far as romantic matters were concerned.

'Ah, Betty, what perfect timing. The cocoa is ready. I know that you dislike the skin of the milk. I admit it looks unattractive, but for myself I like the texture of it in my mouth.'

Betty did not choose to interpret Kenneth's liking for the skin of the milk but was pleased to accept her own cup free of film. She was more than pleased to note that Bertrand was joining them for an evening drink. She had heard his cry from the heart but now noticed that he had filled in some competitions. This indicated that his recovery from emotional decline would be more rapid than usual.

'Shall I post these for you?' She picked up the envelopes as Bertrand could never be relied on to do such things for himself. Effort seemed to be more important than result – or perhaps the results came so long after the effort that one forgot what the original effort was for. Bertrand's long and diligent work in the social services had taught him to accept such things. One couldn't expect rewards.

'It's kind of you, Betty – yes, please post them. I don't suppose that I'll be going out of the house for a time.' Bertrand spoke as though the prospect of fresh air might choke him. He did not wish his spirits to be lifted too quickly.

'Ah, they are all first-class. I'll post them tomorrow.' Betty paused and looked at a piece of paper that had somehow got itself between the envelopes. It read: 'Victor Holder – ring at home after 8 p.m.' She frowned. Bertrand had never mentioned a Victor. 'I don't know who this is?' She held out the piece of paper between her thumb and forefinger as though she were feeding some snapping pekinese dog with a tit-bit.

Bertrand took it from her gently and looked at the name and number with equal puzzlement. Slowly the lines of bewilderment faded from his brow. Indeed, his expression changed into one of gleeful enlightenment. 'It's him. The window-man.' He spoke reverently.

'I beg your pardon. Who did you say?' Kenneth asked.

'It's the new launderette manager, the man that came in through the window. Surely, you cannot have forgotten him already. How kind of him to leave his name and number, wise of him not to mix business with pleasure.' Bertrand placed the address in his shirt pocket as he spoke.

'What pleasure?' Betty asked.

'Well, well – any pleasure, Betty. Just conjecture. It ought not to be difficult to imagine some kind of pleasure with Victor. When he climbed in through the window, I had the feeling that a red-haired invader had entered our home. The dark blue eyes, the flaming hair – all the appearance of a Viking in transit.' Bertrand took a long satisfying drink of cocoa.

Betty had thought that he looked more like a pale-faced, pimple-spotted young man from Harlesden – but then her nature had never been romantic. And the young man *did* have red hair. If Bertrand saw him as a beautiful reincarnate Viking, then why should she worry about it? Kenneth sought to change the subject.

'Now, about tomorrow, Betty. I think that we should leave here at about 10.30 in the morning. I hope that it will remain fine as our trip will take us out of doors.'

'The forecast is fine, warm and dry,' said Betty.

Bertrand was a little perturbed that Kenneth and Betty had not mentioned where they were going. It was true he had said that he himself was not going out of doors. But good friends ought to give one another the option of a change of mind or mood. Bertrand felt excluded and said: 'I'm sorry that you and Betty appear to feel that the quality of your lives should be of no interest to me. I accept sadly that you are both going on a secret trip.'

'Oh, it's not a secret to Kenneth.' Betty laid her hand reassuringly on Bertrand's knee. 'Only to me is it a secret,' she added.

'I have planned a series of Sunday Mystery Tours for Betty. The first of these takes place tomorrow. She is unaware of her destination, or the content of the visit. Of course, Bertrand, you are more than welcome to join us. Would you like a digestive biscuit with your cocoa?'

Bertrand took a biscuit from its cellophane wrapper; he hated surprises but now had no choice but to accept Kenneth's invitation. Mildly paranoid behaviour often found its own punishment in this way.

'Yes, yes, I'd love to come.' He spoke as though he had agreed to attend some distant cousin's wedding. 'I don't know what I shall wear.'

'Wear what you like,' said Betty.

Betty felt that Bertrand had never really worn what he liked; he seemed to dress in order to mirror the persona of the particular partner who was the object of his devotions. Did he do this to please them? It had bought him no long-term dividends – only a wardrobe of discarded clothes looking like a collection from several people when their source had been solely Bertrand.

His last four outfits all seemed to be intent on exaggerating his maleness. At one period he had worn hobnail boots, dirty jeans, a torn shirt and transfer tattoos on his arms. His friend at this time had not been a scaffolder or a hod-carrier but an accountant who wished to resemble a building worker. Betty had once gone into the bathroom and found Bertrand sitting in a bathful of water still wearing his jeans. He had allowed them to dry on him. Every line and contour of his pelvic regions was etched beneath the skin-tight material. His jeans looked as though they had been painted on him. Eventually, two bad attacks of sciatica had put an end to this shrinking exercise.

In turn he had looked like an S.S. motorcyclist (he had never owned or ridden a motor-bike but wore a helmet); a grape-picker (one-piece dungarees and sandals); a racing cyclist (brief shorts, sweatshirt and plimsolls); and a political crusader (shaved head and a chain about his neck). Perhaps all of these friends of Bertrand had something beneath each guise apart from . . .

'As a child I never saw any of my foster fathers in anything except for navy blue or grey suits. They even dug the back gardens wearing a suit. And they polished their shoes every morning. Their shoes always lasted a long time. One of them had his last fatal heart-attack behind the wire grille at the post-office. He was most upset that the counter clerk trying to help him had sought to remove his tie.' Bertrand sighed and added, 'Yet he was a kind man. He always referred to himself as a "servant of the public".' Bertrand drained his cocoa as if he were making a retrospective toast to many such men.

'I'll make packed lunches for all of us. If I get them ready tonight they will stay fresh in the fridge for tomorrow.' This was Kenneth's way of telling everyone that he would like the kitchen to himself.

'I think I'll just make a quick telephone call and have an early night.' Bertrand paused at the door. 'Oh, Betty, I have a couple of kaftan shirts that you might like. I'll put them in your room.'

Betty smiled a thank you. A kaftan shirt might be more

useful than a crash-helmet or bicycle pump, discarded souvenirs. She would go to bed and read her book about Elizabeth Fry's work with fallen women. It might help her to forget the growing pain which seemed to be biting at the centre of her stomach.

'Hello, hello, is that you, Victor? Yes. Remember me? Bertrand. Bertrand – yes, we met here at the flat just . . . yes . . . Well, why not . . . mm–mm I'm free on . . . I don't mind if you . . .' Betty could hear Bertrand's voice in the hallway. Clearly, his total recovery was imminent; she entered her room and took up one of the kaftans from the bed.

She held the garment to her and stood before the wardrobe mirror. No, she could never wear it – not outside, but she might put it on here, in her bedroom, and not look in the mirror. A solitary tear trickled down Betty's left cheek; it was shed, not for herself – but for the garment and what it represented.

Seven

Kenneth Trask found it difficult to sleep. He felt hot and sticky. He lay in bed covered by a single, light cotton sheet. His window was wide open, yet there seemed to be a shortage of air. Nothing could be more eccentric or unpredictable than English weather. It was early May and now from some strange ocean current a heat wave seemed to have been sent to afflict London. He heard Betty cough. He hoped this evening's humidity would not leave her fatigued for the morrow.

When the rumbles of thunder began to reverberate throughout the room, Kenneth rose from his bed and draped the sheet about him like a toga.

He marvelled at the streaks of lightning as they crackled and split the sky. The rain came in an immediate downpour; he saw two women run for shelter in the launderette doorway below his window. The rain stopped less than ten minutes after it had started, but Kenneth was grateful that it had left the air fresh and the sky free of electricity. He could hear one of the women below him talking. She spoke in a flat voice with very little expression. It was like hearing a commentary on the Eurovision song contest or listening to the dead speak.

'There's no way I'm going back to him. I'd rather starve, yes, I'd rather starve than go back to him. My mum says I've made my bed and now I've got to lie in it. Oh no, I'm not lying in that bed any more. This is the last time he is laying his hands on me. The last, I can tell you. Married five years, miscarried twice from him kicking me all over the house. Called the police once – "domestic", that's what they said. It's domestic, is it, to have your stomach kicked in, two stitches over your eye, and then be pulled across the bed and . . .' The woman had begun to cry.

A taxi cab pulled into the kerbside; the older woman gave the driver an address. It began to rain again as the vehicle pulled away. Kenneth retired to his bed. He wondered if that lady's marriage had been blessed by the Church or honoured by the State. Either way, blessings or honours were irredeemably empty.

Kenneth slept happily alone and it was probably a good thing that he did not know that the stranger in his doorway had once more returned to her spouse. And once again, within Holy Matrimony they had made love (of a kind). The man could not comprehend devotion and sadly the woman thought he might not be a real man if he could; it was ignorance rather than neurosis which inflicted the savagery on the perpetrator and the afflicted.

In the meantime Betty dreamed of Miss Trask – how ridiculous to be dancing together on a bowling green? Ought we to be gliding around like this with such gay abandon?

Bertrand's slumbers had taken him back to his childhood. All the staff of the children's home were in the back garden. A tall, angular lady was dead-heading rosebushes. A middle-aged man was tying stakes around a huge clump of delphiniums which were of exotic blue. Bertrand was counting marigold seeds in the palm of his hand. None of this would have seemed at all unusual except that all of the trio were stark naked.

'This is The Nag's Head. We change buses here.' Kenneth ushered his companions along the aisle of the bus.

'London has such extraordinary place-names. There's

Ponders End, Nag's Head, Elephant and Castle, Crouch End . . . They are nothing if not original and one would hardly expect to hear such names anywhere else. They still have a Dickensian ring.' Betty was helped off the bus by Bertrand as she spoke.

The day was warm but not uncomfortable. The storms of the previous night had left the air fresh, except for clouds of petrol and diesel fumes which burst from the backs of great trucks and lorries. Another short bus-ride took our travellers to the entrance of Waterlow Park. Here they drank tea and ate sandwiches; they fed bad-tempered grey squirrels. They visited an aviary which seemed to contain only two desolate looking macaws, and pretended not to see a young man and his girlfriend indulging in their first passions behind a herb-scented garden provided for the blind. It had been Kenneth's idea for the trio to feign blindness. They had linked hands, gazed fixedly ahead as the young man's bottom rose and fell. 'It's OK, they can't see us, love – hold on, I'm nearly there – go on – on –' The smell of verbena, lavender and sage gave the air a spicey and tangy flavour – perhaps it was this aroma that had caused the young couple to be free of caution. Passion could often seem to enter matters without plan. Betty opened her eyes to scan the lake only to find that coots and ducks seemed to be affected too.

'Everything appears to be mating,' said Betty. She wondered whether one should, after all, close one's eyes to such things but made no more comment.

'We only have to wait five minutes or so. There is a guided tour each hour, on the hour. I should think that these other people are waiting as well.' Kenneth's 'surprise' was over as Betty and Bertrand now knew that they were about to embark on a guided tour of Highgate Cemetery. Betty did not find the prospect uplifting and Bertrand felt indifferent. 'I'm sure that we will find a lot to interest us,' Kenneth added.

'Oh, I'm sure.' Betty spoke emphatically.

'Quite unusual. How original of you to think of it, a real surprise for us.' Bertrand sat down on the wall which held the wrought iron fence in position. He noticed that a foxglove had grown and bloomed out of a crack in the mortar. 'The insides of foxgloves resemble the bellies of newts.' He peered into a bell-shaped bloom as he spoke and watched a bee hover and enter.

'If you could all keep together it will certainly help me; now how many are there of you? Seven. Well, yes, I don't think any more people will arrive now, so we can begin.' Their guide announced himself in this manner and by a gentle motioning with his bare left arm, bade the group to follow him.

Kenneth was a little concerned with the man's attire. He had expected a guide in these surroundings to be a little more formally dressed. Why, with the coarse-looking shorts, the off-white singlet darkened by sweat stains under the armpits, the boots with woollen socks turned over the top, he looked as though he were set to climb a mountain rather than tour a cemetery. The group trailed behind him as he led them forward along a gravel path.

The guide's first comment was horticultural rather than historical. He pointed out where various bits of undergrowth had been cut back to reveal gravestones and statues to a former glory of space and light. As monuments, Betty did not think the statues in any way exceptional. Might not they look better covered by ivy and bindweed? She noticed that a couple of blackbirds were nesting in a forlorn looking angel's wing crevice – real shelter midst death.

When the guide did begin to pick out gravestones which he thought of interest, the interest left Betty, Kenneth and Bertrand unmoved. This one belonged to a well-known furniture manufacturer, that one was a sports-kit manufacturer. 'Note the tennis rackets and cricket bats etched in stone.' The other tourists expressed some wonderment over these observations; as their 'oohs and ahs' poured forth, Betty frowned as she looked at the gravestones recording the deaths of children.

There seemed to be whole families stricken with the blight of child-death. So many children dying before they were even ten. She also noticed that some men had more than one widow buried with them. Perhaps two wives out of three dying of childbirth. And these were the wealthy – what of the poor? Ah, those Victorian values! thought Betty – based more on appearance than love. What a rancid legacy they had left behind – moral indignation abounded and was falsely correlated with integrity. Before half the tour was complete Betty felt that she could stomach little more of it.

Ten minutes had been spent in an area where a bomb had dropped during the last war. It was gorily pointed out that one of the vaults nearby was used in the making of Dracula films. Kenneth had become tetchy and irritated when the guide had talked about the Rossettis' tomb without mentioning Christina's gifts.

They had paused in what was termed the Egyptian Section; the guide pointed to a marble slab.

'Ah, this has become a shrine for lesbians and some feminist thinking ladies. A writer called Radclyffe Hall is buried here. She wrote a scandalous book called *The Well of Loneliness* – it upset quite a lot of people as it was about two lesbians who loved one another.'

'Two people. First – first they were two people.' Bertrand's composure had cracked and he shouted above the stillness of the place. The guide and the other visitors were taken aback by the ferocity of his tone. Neither Betty nor Kenneth felt that they wanted to constrain him.

'Their love was . . . their love was re . . .' Bertrand could not find the correct word; his anger impeded his expression.

'Devotional.' Betty spoke quietly.

'The book is in every decent library in the land today. I have read it.' Kenneth looked straight into the face of his guide, held his eyes with a challenging stare and added: 'It is not at all scandalous. In those same libraries you can find scandalous books by any number of well-known heterosexuals. Some are living – some are dead.'

At this point the guide had changed his discourse on to architecture. Radclyffe Hall was left to rest peacefully and Betty, Kenneth and Bertrand decided against visiting the 'shilling burial hall' and made their way back to the entrance gate. When they were eventually let out Betty thanked Kenneth for organising the trip.

'It has been quite an experience.' She said this and meant it; and then, after a few moments of inner reflection, added, 'I want no memorial after my death. I do not wish my name to be carved on any piece of stone, or lead, or lump of wood. I do not wish to be recorded.'

'As you wish,' Kenneth replied and Bertrand nodded agreement.

Kenneth noted that Betty had shuddered involuntarily as she spoke and had clutched her bottle-green cardigan closer to her scrawny body. Dark rain clouds had begun to form in the sky, and chilling breezes had begun to blow.

Fortuitously, a taxi came into sight and stopped nearby to dump a group of further visitors for yet another cemetery tour. The dead could be visited each hour on the hour. They had a better deal than some living patients in hospitals and were often given more respect. Kenneth hailed the empty cab.

He was glad of its appearance. He helped Betty into her seat and let Bertrand get in after her. He climbed into the seat facing them, gave the driver instructions as to destination and closed the door. He was concerned about his own feelings; he had never been demonstrative. And yet . . . and yet . . . when Betty had shuddered and pulled her cardigan about her shoulders, he had wished to hold her to him, to shelter the wretched sparrow-like lady near his body. Offer his warmth to her.

The taxi suddenly swerved and braked and Kenneth was pitched forward into Betty's arms. He extricated himself as the cab almost drew to a halt – the driver pointed to a stray dog safely padding along the pavement. The creature unaware of road-sense sniffed urgently forward in search of an elusive bitch.

'I'm sorry about that, Betty.' Kenneth withdrew to his seat.

'No need to apologise, Kenneth. You cannot accept blame where it is not due. That poor dog seems to be in quite a state. Passion can be a terrible thing.'

Kenneth wondered how Betty could know anything about passion – but Bertrand thought that her observation was correct. The taxi returned to its former speed and sped them homewards without any further incident. Rain had begun to spatter the pavements and roadways but the travellers were all unaware of this inclemency.

As Betty, Kenneth and Bertrand entered their front door, six rain-sodden tourists sheltered inside a vault in Highgate Cemetery and four fledgling blackbirds took their first flight from an angel's wing into an early summer storm.

Eight

'Take off your clothes.'

'Everything?'

'Yes, underwear too. You won't feel cold. Place your clothing in the hanging crate, would you? Leave it in the cubicle. It will be quite safe there. Do come out when you are ready. Miss Hooper, isn't it?'

'Yes, it is. Miss Betty Hooper.'

'Ah yes, I remember.'

'So do I,' Betty muttered to herself as she entered the cubicle. Undressing did not take her very long. She hesitated for a few seconds before finally discarding her knickers.

'No! Leave your underpants on – just a little longer – I like to see the bulge.'

'See me as I am.' Victor disobeyed Bertrand's request and pulled the last garment covering his body roughly away from himself. 'There!' he said and contemplated his own hardness with what could have been some self-satisfaction. 'It's yours.'

Bertrand looked at the ivory coloured human form, the flaming patches of red hair nestled under the armpits, the fiery bush above the appendage which now seemed to stand out incongruously from the thin body. He approached it gently and it appeared to move of its own volition – as if to welcome him.

The doctor smiled professionally before he spoke: 'It is Miss Hooper – of course it is. Been some pain, has there?'

'Yes, quite a lot,' said Betty, whose nakedness caused her to feel somewhat demoralised. Perhaps it was not the nakedness – how could someone who had amputated one of your breasts forget you? But he had remembered. 'Where do you want me?' she asked.

At his request she lay on a leather couch covered by a single sheet. There was no pillow provided and she closed her eyes as she lay submissive and horizontal. His hands moved about her body. 'Can you feel that? Does it hurt? Now, when I do this does it hurt more? Mm . . . Mm . . . Mmm.' She answered his question truthfully but kept her eyes closed. It was as though her brain had disowned her body – there was pain but she somehow managed to stay outside of it. His touch did not stir Betty's imagination in any way. From the neck downwards, for all intents and purposes, she might just as well have been a lump of plasticine.

'There; now, I think we'll have some photographs of you now.' The doctor tapped Betty's knee, signalling her to rise. 'Just put on the green smock – would you? You will find one inside the cubicle.'

'Shall I take my clothes with me?'

'No, it's quite alright to leave them here as I'd like to see you after I've seen the X-Rays.'

Betty reappeared from the cubicle to find the doctor sitting behind a desk with a top supported by tubular steel legs. Betty thought the shining steel looked functional; she sometimes found that what was utilitarian was often unattractive. Yet she could not expect this talented doctor to enter her suffering in order to cure it. This would not be possible . . . there was simply too much suffering in his work. He had put on some spectacles and was writing something on a yellow card.

He handed the yellow card to her. Then she proceeded

to follow a line of orange arrows which led her through a
maze of corridors to a lift. The lift descended and she
followed more orange arrows into the bowels of the
hospital. No one seemed to mind her dark green smock
and she was pleased to see two other ladies similarly attired
in the reception area of the X-Ray Department. A third
lady was defiantly dressed in a sari. All three ladies smiled
sympathetically in acknowledging Betty's presence.

There were no books to read, no magazines to glance
through – the ladies had to wait and fret or wait and dream
in order to pass the time. Eventually, only Betty and the
lady in the sari were left. It was now impossible for Betty
to dream, as her compatriot in pending adversity had
begun to manifest her anxiety by pacing about the room,
wringing her hands and making clicking noises with her
mouth. The bracelets that adorned her wrists clinked and
her green and gold sari floated this way and that – a moth
seeking light, unable to settle. It hovered about Betty
seeking some kind of reassurance.

'It's alright, my dear, they are only going to take a few
photographs. As far as I am concerned my inside cannot
look much worse than my outside – I am sure that you
have nothing to worry about and . . .' The lady had begun
to shake her head from side to side and then spoke in
Urdu; she touched her own lips and then extended her
palms outwards in an expression of exasperation.

'Ah, you don't understand English?' Betty asked.

For reply, the lady nodded vehemently, but fluttered
and gradually settled onto the seat next to Betty.

In her long career as a teacher Betty had found that one
of the last resorts for diminishing tension or stress was to
sing, and if possible to get others singing. Her voice was
thin but not unpleasant and her sense of pitch was nigh on
perfect. If she began to sing now, might not this lady think
that she was mad? Did it matter what the lady thought of
her? If Betty was to help her she could not afford to be

egocentric. (Mrs Goodheart had once proffered her opinion that Betty was irredeemably eccentric.) Betty raised her forefinger and began to sing. Somehow, she felt that *Land of Hope and Glory* or such stirring songs would be of little use in the present situation; the tone and content of such songs could offer neither her new friend nor herself any comfort in their joint anxiety.

'One finger, one thumb, keep moving.' Betty raised her thumb and forefinger as she sang. 'One finger, one thumb, keep moving. One finger, one thumb, keeping moving – let's all be merry and gay.' The lady took up the actions of the swinging rhythm as the momentum and tempo increased. The song had endless possibilities as far as expression was concerned, but even Betty had begun to wonder if she could explore its theme much further.

'One finger, one thumb, one arm, one leg, one nod of the head, stand up, sit down . . .' At this point, when both ladies were laughing and breathless, a smart-looking lady in a white uniform adorned by a badge entered the room.

'Mrs Lal – could you come this way please?'

Mrs Lal had just begun to raise her finger for yet another round of singing. Betty's trill notes faded. Mrs Lal looked towards Betty for reassurance. Betty nodded and pointed towards the lady in white. Mrs Lal followed the lady but gave Betty one pleaful glance over her shoulder as she passed through the swing door. Betty watched the door swing to and fro and finally come to a halt.

She could not muster enough enthusiasm to continue singing the rhyme alone. In any event, there was no longer any part of her body she could fit into the rhyme unless she wanted to be vulgar. And she did not choose to be rude. 'And I who have discovered the universe am reduced to the perimeter of my own body,' Betty quoted Galileo – or a semblance of him. It was a silly thought but she felt she would like to have a chat with him at this time. There was nothing wrong with an imaginary conversation; indeed it would probably be more interesting than a real one.

Just as Betty was about to ask Galileo her first question, a dreadful wailing sound rent the air. It was human, it was near, and it was a real cry of fear or distress.

Bertrand had never heard such ecstatic cries. The language was harsh sounding and emotional. It had been followed by cries of exultation and intermittent sighs which had petered out into gentle breathing.

'Don't move, stay like this for a while. The afterwards is the best part, if what's gone before's been good. Don't move.' Victor whispered his command gently in Bertrand's ear as he lay above him.

'Were you speaking within possession? The words – they were primeval – pagan – I . . . I . . ?'

'Please be quiet now. I was speaking Welsh. I'm from Wales. Now rest with me, with my body. You've had my root and my roots. Lie still. Don't talk yourself out of bed.'

'Miss Hooper, I wonder if we could call on you for assistance. We are having problems with Mrs Lal – er – communication. Do you speak Urdu?' Betty had risen and joined the white-coated lady at the door. The lady seemed to have lost some of her former composure. Another wail came from the other side of the swing door. The white-coated lady brushed a wisp of hair from her brow. 'Oh dear, I do hope you can help us.'

'I'll try,' said Betty. 'But I am afraid I do not speak Urdu – er – speech is only one form of communication – one can signal or empathise or . . .' Betty stopped speaking as she caught sight of Mrs Lal, who knelt in the middle of the X-Ray room with half of her sari wound about her body and the other half making a silken train that disappeared behind a curtained recess.

'We cannot get her to remove her sari; nor can we persuade her to climb into the X-Ray machine. It's quite hopeless. This is the third appointment and the same thing has happened each time. Her family say that she is not to be returned home until the X-Ray is complete. We have telephoned them and they have refused to collect her.' Mrs Lal sobbed as the white-coated lady explained the situation to Betty.

Betty did not find it difficult to enter Mrs Lal's suffering. The machine itself looked bad enough – rather like those dive-bomber ride machines at fun-fairs. The prospect of travel in such a conveyance at any time was appalling but to travel in one when naked had to be much worse. Yet, the X-Rays had to be taken. Betty extended both hands to Mrs Lal who knelt near the machine. The greeting was one that might have been extended to a long-lost loved one. Mrs Lal took Betty's hands into her own and raised herself from the floor.

'I understand your feeling of humiliation – but at such times as this one just has to be brazen. If you are forced to wear a scarlet letter then embroider it beautifully and wear it for all to see. At least the letter is of your own making,' Betty spoke. Mrs Lal did not understand her but she smiled and was not in the least surprised when Betty broke into song. Mrs Lal had never heard *Nymphs and Shepherds* before.

'Nymphs and shepherds come away, come away, come away,
Nymphs and shepherds come away, come, come, come away,'

Betty trilled in a thin, piping voice.

Mrs Lal clapped an accompaniment and began to emulate Betty as she commenced to dance about the room.

'This is a hymn to life – Mrs Lal,' Betty called out as she cast off her green overall and exposed her mutilated and aged nakedness. She continued to sing as she gathered up the loose end of the sari. Mrs Lal twirled around like a top; she giggled and laughed as Betty spun her into nakedness.

'In ye grove, let's sport and play, let's sport and play.' And that is what Betty proceeded to do as she danced around the machine. Mrs Lal copied her actions. If Betty waved her arms as if they were swan's wings, then so did Mrs Lal. If Betty made a bad attempt at moving like a penguin on land then so did Mrs Lal. When Mrs Lal climbed from the machine both ladies collapsed with breathless giggles on the floor.

'Ahem, ahem. Mrs Lal, you had better put on your clothing now.' Mrs Lal was abruptly brought out of her Elysian postures by the white-coated lady's voice. She managed to get up from the floor with as much dignity as she could muster and disappeared behind a curtain, hauling trails of gold and green silk behind her.

'You too, Miss Hooper. We managed to get yours done as well.' The white-coated lady handed Betty the olive-green overall. Betty covered herself quickly – she sensed disapproval.

'Thank you for your help, Miss Hooper. I really don't know how we would have managed without it. It was certainly the most unorthodox piece of counselling or persuasion that I have ever witnessed. You should dress now and return to see the doctor. He will have seen the X-Rays by the time you are ready.' She delivered a short, wintry smile.

'Orthodox! Orthodox! Conform! Conform! What is orthodoxy today is heresy tomorrow – what is conformity now may be . . . may be . . . a nuclear bomb in a minute's time.' Betty was still a little breathless from her dancing and the white-coated lady heard little of what she said. As far as she was concerned it was just one more cranky old spinster – one saw and heard all sorts of things in hospitals. Sometimes one laughed at distress and scorned truth – otherwise one really wouldn't be able to cope.

Still a little fatigued from her previous exertions, it took Betty much longer to dress than usual. Her stockings seemed to want to wriggle into a world of their own rather than settle over Betty's bony feet and ankles. At last, she was ready. She found the doctor once more behind his shiny chrome-legged desk. He smiled more openly than before and Betty was convinced that ill-tidings were her due. He gestured towards the chair: 'Do sit down, Miss Hooper. Please.' He looked down at a file of papers on his desk. He did not raise his eyes as he spoke.

'Now – er – let's see, we saw you – just three years ago?'

'Yes, almost to the day.'

'Then it was a lumpectomy.' He spoke this as if to himself – but Betty answered.

'I was cut, just cut.'

'Six months later it had to be a mastectomy.'

'Mm – mm – the whole breast went.' Betty translated these surgical terms – stating what they were gave her some kind of eerie satisfaction.

The doctor appeared not to hear her; he continued talking to his papers. 'Er – erm – you did have quite a bout of radiotherapy already – there had been some remission – no, we can't give you any more radiotherapy – mm – ah – '. He sighed audibly and looked up from his desk; then unfastened the top button of his shirt and loosened his tie. Betty saw that he looked human; she saw that he was distressed for her and she felt sorry for him.

'I could discuss the idea of some course of chemotherapy with you, Miss Hooper.'

'You could,' said Betty. 'But you won't because you really don't think it would do much for me one way or the other – do you?'

'I'm sorry,' the doctor replied.

'How long?' Betty bent down to straighten her left stocking which had begun to slide down her leg.

'Pardon?'

'Time? Time?'

'One can't be sure of these . . .'

'Please guess.'

'I would say – four or five months.'

'Thank you. You have been wonderfully kind.'

They stood simultaneously. He shook Betty's hand and then, almost as if he were a child spontaneously pleased with a previously little loved aunt, he kissed Betty lightly on her right cheek.

'These tablets, this medicine; there will be no pain . . .' These were his last words to her. Already he had taken some of her pain from her. Not much, but more than she could have expected in such circumstances.

Bertrand insisted on saying something. Victor lay naked next to him. His eyes were closed, but as Bertrand started to speak Victor placed a hand over his already closed eyes as if to shield them from some extraordinarily powerful sunlight. Bertrand looked down on Victor as he spoke.

'It grows faster than a runner bean after flowering. Its nourishment is variable. It can be a source of pleasure, a source of life, a source of illness, a source of crime or a source of shame. It should be treated with care and tenderness. Like everything else it responds to a little loving.'

'If you must talk – talk about "me" or "us" but not "it". As of this moment, I would rather you not talk at all,' said Victor.

Nine

Kenneth often wanted to say all kinds of things to Betty –
but his command of language and natural reticence
forbade him. Nevertheless he did talk to her through his
journal. This had its compensations as she could not
answer him back – and somehow he felt closer to her when
he was writing to her in this way.

Today he had wanted to be very close to her. He knew
what her appointment was about and the prospect of its
prognosis left him in fear and trembling. Kenneth could
not imagine a minute's joy in this life if Betty ceased to
exist. This was why he had sat himself at the kitchen table.
He had placed one of her navy blue cardigans about his
shoulders, he had slid his feet into her slippers, and had
placed her yellow beret on his head. He felt closer to her –
and wrote.

'Ah, dear Betty, it is after 4.30 p.m. and I expected you
back but you have not arrived. I arrived home at 3 p.m. to
find the place empty. I hoovered throughout, did the stairs
and have given the kitchen a good going over. I mention
this as Bertrand seems to have been a little remiss about
domestic details for these past few months. I have
mentioned it to him but he says that I shouldn't even think
of such things. "– Think of D. H. Lawrence and think of
LIFE," he said. All he thinks of is his Victor – there is life
elsewhere too – I told him that Katherine Mansfield did the
washing up whilst Lawrence and her husband talked of

LIFE. I do feel that she might well have wept into the sink. I am certainly not going to weep over Bertrand, though I suspect his new friend Victor may well end up doing just that.

'Bertrand is commencing work at the launderette (mornings only) as from next week. We received an incorrectly addressed letter today for a "Mr Vivian Jones". I will not tell Bertrand Victor's real name as he does not appreciate ambiguities. For my own part I find "Vivian" most charming. I slipped the letter through into the launderette and caught a bus to Finsbury Park. It is one of the few London parks that I have never visited.

'I cannot say that I can recommend it to you. There is hardly a trace of landscape in it. There are acres and acres of fields, corners for young children, tennis courts – but very little for the mature or reflective mind. The flower beds are all instant pot to earth and though colourful appear to have little to do with nature.

'The entrance to the park and the grass immediately around it was littered with human debris. There were at least fourteen men and women sprawled about in drunken stupors and this at 10.30 in the morning. They were not violent or quarrelsome but looked to be shell-shocked or brain-damaged.

'Like everyone else, I walked past them as if I had not seen them – but I was pained by my own studied cut-off from some of my fellow human beings. I thought of this when I was feeding the ducks and got no satisfaction from throwing bits of bread into their squawking bills.

'I left the park by a side exit which was a footbridge over the main railway – on reaching the other side, I noticed that another railway line (long since closed) led north-wards. I decided to explore this disused track. It was indeed most strange as it proved to be full of all kinds of curiosities.

'I came across a fig tree not barren but loaded with fruit.

There were bushes of orange blossom that gave off a pleasant but heady scent, and the walk was marked by the presence of hundreds of butterflies. (I had seen none in the park.) How the buddleia bushes had got there in such profusion I do not know. But they were everywhere – their long, phallic blossoms of purple, red and light blue being a constant source of attraction to the lepidoptera.

'It was most odd walking amidst all this and being able to see chimney-pots and rooftops on either side – one was in the heart of the city but outside of it. A derelict railway station had buddleia growing out of its concrete cracks. The station had lost its name but someone had painted "Shitsville" on the wall.

'Further on, I met two elderly ladies picking blackberries. I joined them for a while expecting them to talk of how this occupation reminded both of them of their lost childhoods. There were no such bucolic memories – they were picking these fruits out of economic necessity. Their local greengrocer paid them 40p a pound and these railway berries went towards supplementing their meagre pensions. They said that the blackberry money would help get them over their winter fuel bill – the buddleia and the butterflies meant nothing to them.

'The railway line ended at Highgate and I walked through into the village. Wealth and poverty are so close in London, there seems little blurring – perhaps our time is Victorian after all.

'I took some tea at a garden centre there and it was served to me in a huge greenhouse that served as a cafe. The atmosphere was hot and humid and trailing plants and creepers hung from the ceiling. I felt as though I were drinking tea in Malaysia.

'It was not Somerset Maugham who spoke to me but a lady whose youngest son had been blinded by something thrown at him by a group of football supporters when the result of the match had displeased them. She was quite desolate but talkative. She talked constantly – eventually she asked me whether I was a football fan. When I replied in the negative she excused herself from the table rather quickly as though for me to be not interested in football was some kind of national sin.

'I wonder if you have ever indulged in sports activities of any kind, dear Betty? I imagine that as a young woman you were thin and lithe – a track runner, perhaps? Sprinter most likely – you certainly could not have had the build for field events – I cannot imagine you holding a great javelin or excelling at water sports . . .'

Betty's exit from the hospital led her through the car park. All over the concrete, sections were marked off for this special person's car or that special person's space. Betty was glad that she did not drive. It seemed to make even the nicest of people officious and bad-tempered. Territorial.

A very loud horn honked and caused Betty to jump, but she did not look in the direction of the noise. She had very little sympathy with drivers who expressed their agitation in such a way. Three more steps and – oh – there it was again – insistent and raucous. She looked to her left from whence the noise came.

A maroon Ford Consul with two men sitting in the front beeped its horn once more. Betty shook her head. She did not know these men. It must be someone else's attention that they were trying to seek.

'Let's spot and plah! Let's spot and plah!'

'In ye grove – let's sport and play,' Betty sang out as she caught sight of Mrs Lal's light brown arm waving a handkerchief from the back window of the car. As she walked towards it a young man got out to greet her.

'We waited for yer. Me mom is in the back. She was tellin' me and me dad how good you were to 'er in there.' He pointed to the hospital building. By now Mrs Lal had got out of the car.

'Spot and plah, spot and plah,' she sang out. She took Betty's hand and Betty hoped that Mrs Lal did not want to demonstrate their previous dance here in the car park.

'She don't have to go there no more. It weren't somefink bad in 'er inside like they thought it were. Me and me dad are right relieved, I can tell yer.'

Could this young man really be Mrs Lal's son? He did resemble her but – 'I was born here,' he said as if divining Betty's mild puzzlement.

'We've been waitin' for yer – just in case yer didn't have transport, like. Me dad's going to run yer home. Mom made him – she's taken a real shine to you. She ain't ever bothered to talk much to anyone outside the family before. I reckon you're the first friend she's met – at least when she's been on her own. I'm Sardinn – but call me Sam.' He proffered his hand.

'Miss Hooper – Betty Hooper – Betty. I'm pleased to meet you.'

'You OK, yerself, then, now?'

'Yes,' Betty lied. 'How good of you to give me a lift home.'

She settled herself into the back seat next to Mrs Lal. She gave Mrs Lal's husband her route home. Mrs Lal held her hand and patted it, and clicked her teeth. The sandalwood perfume circled about them . . . 'How fortunate I have been today,' thought Betty.

'And yet – even when I recall all these incidents, it has been a day of waiting as far as I am concerned. I know where you are and I know that they are looking into your illness. The illness does not seem to worry you at all. Illness does not worry me – but the thought that it might take you away from me leaves me in deep dread – without you here nothing would be wondrous to me. I would not want to stay on this earth if you were not about – but I could never take my own life . . .' At this point Kenneth adjusted the

yellow beret at a more jaunty angle, fastened the top
button of the navy blue cardigan, and pushed his feet
deeper into Betty's slippers. He wrote:

A Tale for Betty Hooper

What great commonplaces are expressed
In poetry, blessed into profundity
by their setting and their sudden pressing forth,
Betty,
In her tuning and turning over and over,
under us, above us, before us
Tells,
enthrals, bewitches, in spangles and myrmidons:
dull, dead, dim,
anxious-spurting darkness
spinning in vortex, weaving wiles benevolently,
beguiling endlessly days and nights away,
patiently progressing, wakingly dreading her hearers,
pointing
from night to light!

After this onslaught of creativity Kenneth dropped his
biro as though it had burned his fingers.

'Oh dear, I've gone over the top. Whatever could have
made me write that kind of . . .' He heard voices coming
from the front door. One of them belonged to Betty. She
was home!

Kenneth assembled himself as quickly as he could. He
hid his journal under a cushion, kicked off Betty's
slippers, removed the cardigan from his shoulders and
hung it on the peg behind the kitchen door. The talking
had stopped and Betty was climbing the stairs. She
entered just as he placed the lid on the enamel casserole
dish with the yellow beret safely nestled inside – out of
sight but in mind.

Betty's spirits seemed high. She recalled her day with

much pleasure and told Kenneth of her good time spent with Mrs Lal. 'And how kind of her family to give me a lift home, wasn't it?'

'Very kind,' said Kenneth. 'And what of . . . what of the results of your examination?' He tried to sound as nonchalant as possible.

'I'm going to die,' said Betty.

'How long?'

'Four – perhaps six months.'

'Oh.'

'I have accepted it.'

'I'll make us a pot of tea,' said Kenneth.

Ten

'Please don't be petulant.'

'I just wished you had mentioned it first, that's all.' Victor put on his anorak and gloves. Mid-September had suddenly gone cold. There had been little gradual switch from the hot summer. There had been no mists, and cold rain had rotted most of the fruit crop. In the five weeks that he had been living with Bertrand, Victor had become more and more homebound. He liked being with and making love to Bertrand. Kenneth fascinated him, and Betty had shown him more courtesy and kindness than he had ever known.

'Ready, then?' he enquired of Bertrand.

'You'll enjoy it when you get there. Diana is such fun and she's dying to meet you.' Bertrand patted his top pocket to make sure that he had his keys.

'I would rather have stayed in. There's a film on television. I was going to sit and watch it with Betty. She looks so drawn and sick today, but she was ever so cheerful-like this morning. I don't want her to die.'

'Please don't mention that anymore. If you accept it, then it will happen. I don't want to think about it. Come on, we'll be late.' Bertrand's tone was sharp.

Victor followed him silently. He wondered why Bertrand refused to face the reality of Betty's condition. Was it that he felt he could help her more by behaving just as he always did? Or was it sheer selfishness on his part?

A 31 bus arrived conveniently. They doubled upstairs and sat in silence. It was not until the bus passed Chalk Farm station that Bertrand shook his head from side to side and placed both hands over his face (as if to hide some ghastly spectacle), then spoke.

'I can't get Betty out of my mind,' he muttered. Victor placed his arm about him and patted his shoulder.

'Keep her in mind, then – keep her there, then. This is Camden Town. We change buses here for Kentish Town.'

Diana Glove poured tiny dribbles of water into her many potted plants. They did not need water but the exercise itself gave her some kind of abstracted satisfaction. She nipped the dead flowers off the pink geraniums and picked two ripe but miniscule tomatoes off a plant which appeared to specialise in producing a dwarf variety of fruit.

Her kitchen, apart from one wall and the floor, was virtually a greenhouse stuck on the street-side wall of her second floor flat in NW5. There was a sizeable lounge, a tiny hall, a bathroom and toilet, and a bedroom that could hold a double-bed and fitted wardrobes. She had quibbled with the estate agent's description of it as a 'luxury'. He had blinked over his steel-framed spectacles and said: 'But consider the area, madam – it's very "in" now.' Although the mortgage repayments of the flat left her almost penniless at the end of each month, Diana felt better in than out. But at 36, she did not enjoy living alone.

'Who is going to look after me?' she would wail in comic distress during her late twenties.

'Oh darling, don't worry,' Bertrand would console her in an empty way, knowing full well that she was more than capable of looking after herself. It was she who wanted to look after somebody else. Social work, institutional care, was simply not enough for her.

They had met when both had worked as young social workers in one of the poorer of the Inner London Boroughs. They had both been (and probably still were) idealistic and industrious. Diana had repeatedly declared to Bertrand that she was without ambition and that control or power, no matter how democratic, would corrupt her perceptions. She was not interested in advancement. Bertrand could not plot his own destiny with such authority at such an early stage in his career, and had remained silent at these times.

Now, a dozen years later, Bertrand worked in a launderette and did occasional 'voice-overs' and Diana was an area team leader of a group of social workers in an Outer London Borough. They remained good friends and would meet once a fortnight to offer minor support to one another with regard to the vicissitudes of people who were treating them unfairly, with regard to artistic enthusiasms of the moment, and with regard to men. Sometimes they quarrelled and at least on two occasions Diana had struck Bertrand.

'You must see this film,' she had said.

'I don't think that I can – not this week – and it's coming off on Saturday.'

'But you must – you must! It's about Flamenco Dancing . . .'

'I don't like Flamenco Dancing – all that stamping and clapping.'

'Don't be sarcastic with me.'

'I don't like Flamenco.'

'How dare you raise your voice to me!'

'I cannot enter all your enthusiasms. I cannot enjoy all the books you read, all the films you see, all the men you . . .'

At this point Diana had slapped Bertrand's head and he had keeled over and fallen from his stool in the wine bar. When he did not move and lay sprawled and still on the floor, Diana had knelt down and rested his head in her lap.

Bertrand recovered when he heard her weeping and saying, 'Forgive me, darling – please forgive me.' He did forgive her but said that he would never meet her again if she wore the heavy silver wrist bangle. She fingered the

bump on the side of his head and discarded the ornament
for life.

Over the years she had introduced five of her men
friends to him and he had introduced eight of his men
friends to her. She felt that none of his male friends were
good enough for him and he felt that none of her male
friends were good enough for her. Once, in desperation,
when the two of them had been jilted and wronged
simultaneously, they had gone to bed together. They
kissed and touched and felt; Bertrand was moved by the
tenderness but not aroused. Diana had licked the inside of
his ear and whispered, 'Don't worry, sweet, it's good
being together. You shouldn't squeeze a marshmallow
into a money-box.' Since this time, they could cuddle one
another (they did this more in public than in private) and
feel secure.

But as the casserole bubbled gently in the oven, and the
autumn cauliflower heads simmered on in the saucepan,
Diana did not feel secure. Domesticity offered little
comfort for her, even if she did have guests coming. Diana
was without a partner, and much as they badly treated her,
she was happier with one. Her plants had done well this
year – she always gave them more attention when she slept
alone. Bertrand was arriving with his Welsh friend. He
was living with him. This had not happened before.
Things had never gone quite that far. Was Bertrand really
in love? Or had he gone mad? Or both? Diana sighed
involuntarily: 'Ah, for a little madness.' From her glass
eyrie she saw the green mini-car squeezing a space for itself
to park in the road below. Her other guests had arrived.

Diana rubbed her chin reflectively as she watched the
passengers climb from the car. The young man handed the
young woman two bottles of wine. There appeared to be
some kind of discussion; the woman was shaking her
head. Eventually she returned one bottle to the man who
locked it away in the car's boot.

It had been an impulse that had caused Diana to invite Felicity to dinner. The girl was working with Diana as part of her placement during her social work training course. Diana had found her pleasant – if a little intense at times. It was after looking at a few instances of injuries perpetrated on children by their parents that Felicity had burst into tears.

Diana had comforted her immediately.

'Come for dinner on Thursday night. Give yourself a break. Bring a friend if you wish.'

'How lovely, I'd love to.' Felicity's acceptance was rapid as was her recovery. 'I'll bring my boyfriend – he's called Mike,' she had added.

'I have a friend coming; he used to work with me some years ago. I think that you will like him. He's most refreshing and often very funny.' Diana had felt a little guilty about referring to Bertrand in this way. He was much more to her than a court jester. And yet she had continued in the same vein. 'He's gay. I hope you don't mind.'

'Oh no, not at all. Mike's uncle is gay. I've met him twice and he's an absolute gas.'

'A what?' Diana had asked.

'A gas. He's funny. He makes us laugh.'

Diana watched the young couple mount the steps of the house. She had not mentioned to Bertrand that other guests were coming. She regretted this now but it was too late to change things. Her generous impulses had often led her into minor duplicities of this kind. Bertrand had once said that considered generosity was . . . The bell rang twice and Diana descended the stairs.

'I'm afraid it's only good old "Vin de Table". Just a trickle from that great wine lake in Europe but you know how funds are when one is a student. Still, it's nice chilled.' Felicity handed Diana the bottle of wine. Diana settled her guests in the lounge and returned to the kitchen. She placed the wine in the fridge and called out. 'Are you a student too – Mike?'

'He's in computing,' Felicity called back.

Diana wondered whether the bottle in the boot of the car was from the wine lake too and whether Mike was dumb. She was relieved to hear him speak when she re-entered the room.

'I love the way you've planned this room. It's got comfort and space – how sensible to eat in the bay window aperture – is that a Hockney print?'

'No, it was one of London Transport's better advertisement posters.'

'What was it advertising?'

'A trip to the countryside, I think,' Diana replied.

'Mm – mm – mm – I'll reserve judgement till later. I like to absorb things before I pass them.' As he spoke Mike gazed into Felicity's green eyes as though he were absorbing her. She gazed back at him and stroked his knee.

Although Mike had been addressing her, Diana suddenly felt redundant. It seemed as though she were not really present. 'I'll go and toss the salad,' she said as the young couple continued to stare at one another.

Some ten minutes later when Diana introduced Bertrand and Victor to her younger guests, Mike managed to shake hands with them but kept his free arm tightly about Felicity's waist. 'I'm Mike,' he said. He sounded like a disc-jockey who firmly believed all the world adored him.

'I'm Felicity – but call me Flea, everybody calls me Flea,' she said.

'There's no spare flesh on her, you see,' Mike patted Felicity's tiny bottom. 'But I love what's there.' Felicity giggled and gazed once more, and Diana, whose figure was more than ample, suggested a glass of sherry.

'It's very kind of you to invite me – not knowing me, like. As Bertrand bought the wine, I got you some chocolates. You do like chocolates?' Victor asked.

'I love chocolates.' Diana took the box from him. 'I shall eat them in bed while I read. How thoughtful of you.' She poured her guests a generous measure of sherry and placed the box of chocolates on the mantelpiece. She was touched by this shy young man's naivety and awkwardness.

Mike observed that Victor was Welsh ('I can always recognise a dialect') and then began to regurgitate jokes which made out every Irishman to be an idiot or every Scotsman to be mean. His attempts at emulating the different accents caused Bertrand to wince. Felicity seemed enraptured. Diana chose to look at her guests and pay as little attention as possible to what was being said. She did not find this difficult.

Bertrand had put on a little weight but he looked relaxed and well. His dark eyes looked less haunted and sad. She noticed that flecks of white hair now peppered his moustache. He wore black corduroy trousers and a navy blue polo-neck pullover. He looked as if he might have just come in from the back garden. Anybody's back garden!

No contrast was added by Victor's clothing – jeans and a black high-necked jumper. No indication of fashion or trend showed anywhere. The auburn hair made his face look paler than it probably was – there were pimples on the forehead and left cheek. The eyes were blue. The top lip had a fringe of orange down that had never been allowed to form a moustache. He was tall and lean and hunched his shoulders as though he were making a permanent apology for his height.

In contrast, Mike was decorated like some male peacock out on the street. His brown hair glittered with blond streaks; his left ear held a tiny jewel in the centre of its lobe. And was there a touch of kohl about those light brown eyes? The expensive black leather bomber jacket was left open to reveal a tee-shirt with a picture of Marilyn Monroe printed on it. But would that lady have wanted to rest her head on that chest? So what does a gay person look like? Diana smiled at her own thoughts.

'I thought you would like that one.' Mike mistook Diana's reflective smile for a response to his joke.

'Pardon? Oh – oh – yes. Very funny. Let's eat. Do sit around the table. Place yourselves where you like.' She accepted Victor's offer of help with transferring food from the kitchen.

Even if Diana's guests had been corpulent, which they were not, there would have been ample seating space for five people around Diana's large Arthurian dining table. She observed that there was far too much space for Felicity and Mike, who had pushed their dining chairs together; they were now close enough to feed one another, and if they got too forgetful there might even be a danger of placing their food in the wrong mouth.

'Please help yourselves.' Diana regretted saying this as Mike followed her request. Generous measures of cauliflower and jacket potatoes were heaped on his and Felicity's plates. The chicken casserole (done in honey and soya sauce) looked badly ravaged as Mike talked and scooped. It was Victor who saved embarrassment for all by declaring that he was moving towards vegetarianism and that he only wanted vegetables and sauce. Bertrand knew this to be a lie and Diana noted that Victor was not without sensibility as well as being courteous.

'Cheers.' Mike raised his glass as though he were some company director who was directing a celebration after a successful deal.

'Absent friends,' said Victor.

'To Betty!' Bertrand spoke quietly but drained half of his wine.

'How is Betty? I do like her,' said Diana.

'She is very ill,' said Bertrand.

'I like her too, you know she is so good to me. It's a

terrible, terrible thing to see her suffer as she does, but she never complains. And her being as ill as she is, it's no sacrifice being with her. I enjoy her company and . . .' Victor was cut short.

'Ah well, it comes to us all sometime,' Felicity murmured wistfully and moved her hand from Mike's thigh to settle it lightly on his crotch. In changing the course of the conversation she also managed to place a death sentence on Betty. Mike removed a chicken bone from his mouth and pecked Felicity on the forehead.

'You're very much alive now,' he said and she answered by pressing a little harder on the inside of his thigh.

Bertrand began to wonder whether this young couple would eventually consume one another before his very eyes. They were lovely to look at but he found it hard to view them as human. It was like sitting down to dinner with two beautiful boa constrictors. They consumed everything before them: food, conversation, wine. How much more could they absorb before they finally began to constrict? By the time that cheese and coffee were served they were coiled about one another.

'I feel so relaxed here, Diana.' Felicity stroked the back of Mike's head with one hand and placed the other one underneath the neckline of his tee-shirt. He opened his legs a little wider so that her pert little bottom could sink more snugly onto his genitals. It was clear that they both intended to stay on longer than Bertrand and Victor. Diana felt cheated but there was nothing she could do.

With some mutterings about an early morning shift Bertrand and Victor made their excuses for leaving. Diana was glad that the two of them had chosen not to 'entertain' her other guests. She felt an affinity with Bertrand that she had not experienced before – social patronage was an unpleasant thing to receive.

'You have something stuck on your moustache. Is it a bit of cauliflower?' Victor asked of Bertrand as Diana handed them their coats. 'Come here. Stand under the light,' he commanded and Bertrand obeyed. Diana was puzzled and her other guests stopped talking. Victor dropped his raincoat to the floor. He placed his arms around Bertrand and drew him tightly to him. He felt Bertrand's discomfort but offered threat rather than help.

'Respond! You respond to me now.' He whispered into Bertrand's ear. 'I love you. I'm saying it now, but if you don't respond, I shall leave you. I mean it. See!' Bertrand accepted Victor's passionate kiss underneath the full glare of the light above them. Felicity's bout of coughing did not terminate their embrace. It was long and full and without compromise.

Mike did not manage to say goodnight and Felicity nodded a relieved goodbye.

'Well now, shall we have another cup of coffee? We can make some fresh now that the boys in the band have left. What did the two lady tennis champions say to one another?' Mike asked of Felicity and Diana.

'I don't know,' said Diana desolately.

'Les be friends,' he chuckled and Felicity tittered.

'If you don't mind, I'd rather go to bed. I have a bit of a headache. I can't seem to shake it off. It's been with me all day. You didn't bring top-coats, did you?' Diana had already begun to gather the coffee cups together.

'That's what happens to career women. Do you think she is experiencing an early menopause? We can drink the other bottle of wine when we get home.' Felicity clicked her seat-belt as Mike turned on the car-radio. He glanced into the overhead mirror – he was not looking for traffic behind him but just checking that he looked alright. He was well pleased with what he saw.

Eleven

Two weeks of cold and rainy weather did not stop Kenneth from viewing the forthcoming holiday with optimism and pleasure. Mid-October spent in the north-ern extremes of England would not be everyone's ideal of vacational bliss. The wind which sent driving sheets of rain spattering against the kitchen window gave him little cause for concern. He wet his forefinger with his tongue, tested the heat of the electric iron and began to smooth out any wrinkles still lurking around one of Betty's blouses. When Kenneth had asked Betty if he could iron her clothes, she had been a little hesitant. 'But I would enjoy it,' he had persisted. Now Betty was grateful for his persistence. It was important for her to conserve her energy. Bertrand had added that Kenneth could do his ironing too, if he wished, but Kenneth seemed not to hear his request.

He had not turned a deaf ear to all Bertrand's sugges-tions. The forthcoming holiday which would send Betty, Kenneth, Bertrand, Victor and Diana to Lancaster for a week had come from Bertrand's inspiration.

An ex-lover of Diana who had been lecturing in English and living in Stoke Newington had left East London to take a job at a College in the North West. Diana, feeling that old wounds were better than none at all, had contacted him and asked if she might stay in his small stone house for a week. His response had been cool but kind. 'Of course, come from the 20th to the 27th. You can have the place to yourself. I shall be away that week. There is plenty to see up here.'

For someone who lectured on the 'Romantic Tradition in Literature', Diana had felt that Bill Bluelea's treatment of her request was a little unimaginative. Yet, she had found herself saying, 'Yes, fine, can I bring a friend?'

'If two share a bed, the place sleeps five,' Bill had replied.

Diana had contacted Bertrand and suggested she join forces with his household. They could all travel in Diana's station-wagon. Betty had agreed enthusiastically. For some reason she wished to revisit Morecambe (a place she had known some years ago). Kenneth and Victor had both welcomed the idea of a week away from London. Kenneth picked up another of Betty's garments. He was testing the strength of the elastic and smiling at the delights that the impending trip might bring when Betty came into the kitchen. She expressed no surprise when a pair of her knickers catapulted from Kenneth's hand across the kitchen and landed in the sink. He retrieved them without comment.

'I don't really want to go,' said Betty.

'Oh, I'm sure a change of landscape, a little sea air . . .'

'No, no, not our holiday. I wish we were going tomorrow instead of next Monday. It would give me an excuse for getting out of this.' Betty placed a letter on the ironing board for Kenneth to view. It read:

> *'The Eaves',*
> *189 Dunhill Road,*
> *London N1*

Dear Miss Hooper,
I am sure that you will be sad to hear that Mrs Goodheart will be leaving us this half-term. You, of all people, must

know of the hard work and effort that she has put into the school for the past five years. Past and present staff and children have much cause to be eternally grateful to her and I am sure that she will be sorely missed.

However, her wings are not being clipped, indeed, she is spreading them further, as she has been appointed to be an H.M.I. of our country's schools. Their gain is our loss, I am afraid, but we are glad that her skills and dedication will now have a wider deployment.

The governors have decided to give her a farewell presentation gift on the evening of the 19th at 7.30 p.m. Wine and Buffet will be served and we are expecting a large gathering.

I would particularly like you to attend as we made no official recognition of your own $31\frac{1}{2}$ years service at this school. This was a little remiss of us and we would like to formally acknowledge your contribution – just a minute or so taken from the main proceedings – probably before they begin. I do hope that you are able to come.

> Yours sincerely,
> Mabel Bevis, OBE,
> Chairman of Governors.

P.S. I am afraid that we no longer award a gold watch for 25 years service or over – ah, these are stringent times – but we have come by a set of golf-clubs which Mrs Goodheart said would be most suitable for you.

Kenneth switched off the iron before he passed the letter back to Betty. He would have liked to have stroked her head, but he did not. Instead he said: 'I think that you should go. I think that we should all go.'

'We will, then,' said Betty. 'I can sell the golf-clubs. The money can fund our holiday – I think that they originally belonged to your sister.'

'Did my sister play golf?'

'No, but one of her close friends did – at least she

sounded as though she might have done – it was all such a long time ago – but I do remember that your sister was especially happy during that period. Your ironing is so beautiful, Kenneth. I won't take tea now. I think that I'll lie down and read for a while. I have never liked being in the rain but I like the sound of it if I am reading.'

Kenneth felt worried. It was unlike Betty to be lying down at 11.30 in the morning. He had noticed that she was walking more slowly and that she ate less. Also, she had excused herself from games of Scrabble prematurely. This had left him and Victor to finish a game that no longer mattered. Her presence, it seemed, was important to everyone.

Bertrand, Victor and Kenneth were all agreed that Betty's farewell should not take the form of a whimper in contrast to Mrs Goodheart's bang. The best justice like the best education was often informally given.

'Ah, is that Mrs Mabel Bevis, OBE? The excellent chairman of the governors, I believe? Yes. I am an ex-pupil of Miss Hooper's – yes, she taught me many years ago. Yes, longer than I can care to remember – mmm – mm – yes – very sad. I wonder if you would mind if I said a little something on her behalf at the leaving reception. Just a few words at the beginning?'

'It would be a splendid idea – but please keep it short. In fact, I'm so pleased that you have made the offer as it could have been a little delicate for me. Yes, I don't think that I could speak, actually, as I am really there for the main proceedings. Yes, if you say a little something it will not detract attention from the platform. Yes, just a few appreciative words – we need not even place it on the programme. Thankyou! Goodbye.'

Bertrand did not feel that he had deceived Mabel Bevis, OBE. He had never been a pupil of Betty's in a state school but she had taught him quite a lot outside of it. What had she said yesterday? 'I suppose that I am now a hedge-school teacher. Only there are no hedges in the city, are there?' Sometimes, Betty's riddles were too much for Bertrand. Yet Victor never seemed perplexed by anything that she said. Apart from work and bed, Victor seemed to spend more time with Betty than with him. Bertrand did not complain. He had never felt so calm as he did during this present time.

As Victor packed the effects carefully into the back of Diana's estate car, he heeded Bertrand's words carefully. 'Even the best speeches can be enhanced by a little drama, a trace of effect – it's just like a production.' Bertrand had rehearsed all of them for the evening's proceedings. Victor supposed that he had been nominated a kind of stage-manager. He was pleased to offer support for Betty and he found it odd that he should be returning to school to do it. He had not visited a school since the day that he left one – and that must be – yes, twelve years ago.

He remembered himself as a pale, tidy boy, who hated being called 'Ginger' – the colour of his hair at this time had caused him some undeclared distress. He had been the last child born of a family of five children. His coal miner father had not been a Catholic, nor had his mother. They had merely enjoyed having children. That is – they had enjoyed having the first four children – two boys and two girls with approximately eighteen months separating each birth. It had been a tidy family – and then, when the family was all but adult – and one daughter and one son were married with children of their own – then, just three months before her forty-fifth birthday Victor's mother delivered him. From the second that he was born he was an uncle.

By the time he was 7 all of his brothers and sisters were married. At 53 his mother was tired. She enjoyed being a grandmother more than a mother ('I like to see the children from time to time.') Victor's pale looks and grave expression did not endear him to his father – who often referred to him as a 'change' baby.

Change seemed to be what his life was about for the next ten years. His parents had simply lost interest in upbringing and Victor was passed along the line of immediate relations. The family cobweb did not spin too far. It was quite simple for him to spend a year with this sister or that brother. His mother, on most occasions that she saw him, greeted him with less affection than she did her grandchildren. She would cuddle them and greet them effusively but somehow Victor always stood apart. He was never held. 'And how are you then, Victor? All right then? Being good to Molly are you?' She would ask these questions as he left with his different assortments of nieces and nephews. He never answered as his mother did not expect a reply.

It was different with Betty. Victor found that Betty listened to him more than anyone ever had before. Somehow she managed to get him talking about things that he had only thought about. He had stored up a lot of unspoken thoughts. 'The cat got your tongue?' his mother would say as he had sat silent during fixed family Christmas revelries. This would only make him more withdrawn and silent. But there had been none of that with Betty. Sometimes they would share their thoughts with words. And (and this Victor found incredible) they could say things to one another without speaking.

It was true, Betty was fond of Bertrand and Kenneth but she declared her love differently for each of them. Surely it was love? She always praised and encouraged Bertrand who could go into ecstasy or the doldrums over the smallest of rewards or the smallest of disappointments. She and Kenneth related to one another as though they were close celibate church dignitaries. 'I'm the only one she touches,' Victor thought as he fastened down the boot of the station-wagon.

Of late, Betty would take Kenneth's arm for assistance on short walks, but she did not ruffle his hair, or place a comforting arm about his shoulder. Nobody had ever touched Victor with affection before – perhaps Bertrand did, but then, that often led to other things.

It was Diana and Bertrand who came out from the front door first. As usual, Diana was attempting to direct operations. Bertrand let her arrange the seating in the car (after all it was her car), but when she began to suggest who should sit where when they got to the school, he had raised his hand in a papal manner. 'Diana, please, please leave that side of the evening to me. I have rehearsed it all with Kenneth, Victor and Betty. All cues are worked.'

'Oh, very well,' Diana shrugged but decided that this was not the time for a row. 'You look very smart, Bertrand – he does, doesn't he, Victor?'

'He always looks smart to me.' Victor grinned as he spoke.

'When you have both finished talking about a pronoun who is me – you might call out to the other two that we are ready,' said Bertrand who was in one of his efficient moods.

'They're here,' said Victor who was the first to observe Betty emerge from the doorway holding Kenneth's arm.

Bertrand drew in his breath. He was taken by surprise. This was odd as clothing rarely surprised him, having worn so many different garbs himself. Kenneth had hired a dress suit which fitted him to perfection. With his grey hair, his light blue eyes and the black and white formality of his clothing, he looked like a civic dignitary or a mature American actor who had taken up politics in a final attempt to win an Academy Award of one kind or another. But it was Betty's demeanour which had caused Bertrand's short intake of breath.

A full-length, black evening dress with a high ruffle-type collar covered her body. She wore silver shoes, and an orchid pinned near one of her shoulders. A simple, tasteful gown with just a hint of adornment . . . but . . . Bertrand repressed the urge to say anything about Betty's appearance. But why was she wearing a yellow beret? Cocked at such a jaunty angle too. It wasn't a pale yellow beret, but an acid-yellow beret with a longer tail than was usual placed in its centre.

Twelve

A great part of the school had been built in the mid 1870s when the first school boards had insisted that the masses should receive some education or inculcation (it depended on how one interpreted such things). Since then, bits and pieces had been added on, so that now the building was a permanent historical testament to institutional architecture. The school hall (which also served as a gymnasium, a drama studio, and a church) was added in the early Sixties. The architect had stressed that the building materials themselves were responsible for its aesthetic appeal. At the time of its opening its raw, unfinished appearance had caused some dismay and concern. Concerns were dismissed as philistinism. Since that time, the roof of the building had leaked during every winter.

Not one of the two hundred or so assembled people thought to question Victor as he placed small speakers about the hall and fitted plugs into sockets. There were no queries about the contents of the large cardboard box or the wickerwork basket shaped like a coffin.

Attention was mainly drawn to the long trestle tables on which were displayed various savoury pastries, salads, cold meats and cheeses. There were sparkling glasses ready to be filled with red or white wine. All this was to be consumed for free – but after the speeches. Stomachs rumbled but people smiled valiantly and made complimentary remarks about the flower arrangements and the decorated wall-bars.

'I don't understand this theme,' said Kenneth as he looked at the cut-out painting on the wall-bars. 'It's not Saint Valentine's Day, is it? There are certainly lots of hearts – all sizes, all colours. That collage is most striking.' He pointed to five heart shapes that had been placed to form a multi-coloured primrose. 'But I don't understand why . . .'

Betty interjected and resolved the mystery for her friends.

'They represent Mrs G-Heart. Heart. Got it?' Betty sighed. 'I think that we had better take our seats.'

'No need to rush. In fact we can wait until everyone else is settled. Our seats are reserved,' said Bertrand, who had now lost interest in the decorations. 'We are in the front row.'

'Do they have our names?' Diana asked.

'It says "official" on all of them, an empty word for an empty chair. I'm sure that our places are secure,' said Bertrand as he watched the throng taking their places. It was not until everyone was settled and the platform party had seated themselves that Bertrand led his group down the central aisle. There was some muttering from the audience as these VIP's took their places. Was the lady in black a past Education Minister? No, it could not be Ellen Wilkinson. One couldn't count Florence Horsborough. Some guests eventually decided that she was some French cultural attaché. She had to be foreign. There was a chic air about her.

From the platform Mrs Goodheart beamed her laser-smile. The sight of Betty – and 'sight' was the right word – caused her to finger her pearl necklace. It was unusual for Mrs Goodheart to display any public anxiety. Mrs Bevis, OBE, rose and thanked everyone for coming. 'Er – ahem – before we embark on our official proceedings,

I would like to take up just a fraction of your time with a short item from the floor.'

Bertrand stood. He had no intention of speaking from the floor. 'Thank you,' he said, and then left his seat, climbed the steps of the platform and stood directly in front of Mrs Goodheart, thus obscuring her from public gaze. He coughed. Victor took this first cue. He switched on his tape and canned applause sounded out. This was joined by applause from the floor and proved to be quite deafening. Victor faded it appropriately and Bertrand began.

'I am an ex-pupil of . . .' Bertrand glanced at his notes and decided to discard them. He would enjoy it more if he left it all to the inspiration of the moment. 'I'm sorry.' He began again.

'If we look about us tonight – and I would ask all of you to do just that – we can see that there are all kinds of hearts. There are warm hearts, cold hearts, faint hearts, lion hearts, broken hearts, transplanted hearts, weak hearts, sacred hearts, bleeding hearts.' (Pause.) 'And now we have a good heart.' (Applause.) '– And that is why I am here tonight – to celebrate a truly good heart. To celebrate Miss Betty Hooper.' (Applause.)

'George Tomlinson, an education Minister who appeared to be interested in education, summarised the worth of Miss Hooper when he said: "The teacher is the vital link. At a pinch you might be able to do without the local education authority, but if there were no teachers, the world would be back to barbarism within two generations."' Bertrand was forced to pause at some length at this point as the audience, which consisted largely of teachers, applauded themselves.

'And there is no one who has remained such a bastion of civilisation throughout increasing barbarism than Miss Betty Hooper who has completed thirty-one and a half years service, three of them with Mrs Goodheart – and what is more – Miss Hooper is still alive and with us today.' (Applause.) 'Do you know that when Miss Hooper first began teaching there were no less than 51 pupils in her class – and that on her last day of teaching she taught 14 children for a whole day in a cloak-room. Consider these strides in education. Are they forward or are they merely two steps to the side?' (Applause.) 'I hear that this year they are running Management Courses for people who organise Management Courses.' At this point Bertrand turned to address the platform.

'He missed his vocation,' Diana whispered to Betty.

'I don't think that he did. Vocation? Nuns have a vocation – a vocation for disinterested love for the world and absolute love for Christ. I cannot say that Bertrand has missed his voca – but, sh–sh.' Betty placed a finger over her own lips as Bertrand began extemporising once again.

'Did you know that there are now more people managing teachers than there are teachers?' Bertrand faced his main audience to be greeted by applause and laughter. He sensed that some were ready for rebellion. If you pissed against the wind – and at times, there really was no choice – at least you could only be spattered with your own dirt.

Diana felt invigorated as she noticed the effect that Bertrand's words were having on the platform. Yet she did not feel entirely comfortable herself. She took a handkerchief from her handbag and patted away the perspiration bubbles that had begun to erupt on her nose and brow. 'You enjoy being a team leader because you can spend hours on the telephone. You have always had telephonitis.' Bertrand had said this during one of their many rows. It was true. And now she talked away into a mouthpiece for hours and was paid for it. Sometimes what she heard and what she said had little to do with what she was paid for. She watched Bertrand now as he collected an old bag of golf-clubs from the corner of the stage as though he had been making presentations of this kind all his life. He lifted one of the clubs out of its resting place and held it aloft.

'But tonight, we are here to celebrate a career that would have none of that – a career as a teacher – a career in the front line. Ladies and gentlemen – it is my privilege – my joy to present these clubs to Miss Betty Hooper.' Victor took his second cue. The tape-recorder sang out 'Nymphs and Shepherds' – a huge number of voices seemed to be singing, and then the large cardboard carton was opened and thirty or forty coloured balloons floated up into the air. The audience clapped as Betty (leaning on Kenneth's arm) climbed the platform steps and received her long-service reward.

Victor was worried. This was his third cue and he was finding it difficult to fulfill his duties. The cane catch on the wicker basket had snapped off in his fingers when he tried to open the lid. He pulled and tugged but the basket lid remained firmly attached. Diana had bounded on to the platform and presented Betty with a bouquet of red roses which she graciously handed over to Kenneth. The platform party were forced to join in the applause although their hands felt like lead. The balloons bobbed in the air and Betty finally returned to her seat as the last shepherd and nymph had finally come away.

Mabel Bevis had expected the hum and buzz of conversation to stop as she rose to introduce Mrs Goodheart, but the air was full of frivolity and repressed revelry. There was laughter – not polite laughter, but semi-hysterical laughter. She was forced to be authoritarian.

'Could I have silence for the platform, please.' She clapped her hands. 'Silence, please. Thank you. Could I have silence for the platform. Silence.' She coughed to test her success and was satisfied. Originally, she had intended to make an introductory speech on behalf of Mrs Goodheart. Time was now short. She felt that the audience were becoming restive, mainly because they were very hungry and some were definitely in need of alcoholic sustenance.

'Now we come to the main proceedings. Our dear headteacher is leaving us. Good by name and good by nature, she needs no introduction from me as she is known to you all – let her speak.' Mrs Bevis gestured by bowing slightly in Mrs Goodheart's direction and sat as Mrs Goodheart stood. There was subdued applause.

A sharp cracking noise resounded through the hall as Victor finally managed to prize the basket lid open.

'I am so pleased . . .' Mrs Goodheart's words died on her lips as a flock of pigeons flew up into the air and circled about above the audience and platform. She stared in disbelief as two or three circled above her, before one finally perched on a rafter directly over her head. Mrs Goodheart was in favour of original presentation but someone would suffer for this. She began again.

'I am so pleased . . .' There was an explosion as one adventurous pigeon decided to peck a balloon. The remnants of the balloon and a stunned pigeon fell on to the audience below.

'I am so pleased . . .' Mrs Goodheart yelled. There was another bang, another stunned pigeon. Mrs Goodheart opened her mouth to speak again. Something struck her bottom lip. Was it rain? She looked down to see her bright blue dress spattered with pigeon shit. She tugged nervously at her seed-pearl necklace and watched the pearls scatter to the floor as the thread snapped.

A large group of pigeons now took flight and wheeled about the hall, before settling and attacking the trays of food on the tables at the back. Three or more pigeons circled about Mrs Goodheart's head as they attempted to feed off pearls. Mrs Goodheart screamed. Mrs Bevis felt that proceedings were beyond recovery and led her group off the platform through the side exit.

People had left their seats and had begun to help themselves to wine. Some were actually feeding the wretched pigeons by hand. None now seemed aware of Mrs Goodheart's presence. She sat on the floor of the platform and managed to raise her head as a last attempt at regaining some kind of dignity. Through a flurry of wings, she thought she saw a yellow beret bowling across the room like some ancient discus. It was coming towards her. Mrs Goodheart closed her eyes and kept her head.

Thirteen

As she reached the edge of the canal bank Diana paused to look at her reflection in the water. She viewed herself critically. As a young woman, a generous person might have described her as vivacious and curvaceous – a less generous person would have described her as plump and vivacious. 'Now, I'm just plump,' Diana thought. She smiled wistfully. She continued to look into the water; a faint ripple dispersed, as did the breeze that caused it.

'What are you doing here?' Diana spoke to the reflection that had now joined hers in the water.

'You have never greeted me like that before.'

'No, I usually throw my arms about you and ask if you have missed me,' said Diana, still talking to the reflection.

'Well, you can do that if you want to. I would like you to do it.' Bill Bluelea did not move from his stance which was just a foot or so behind her.

'I don't want to,' said Diana. 'I am tired of enthusing at the sight of you. I thought you were away. You said you wouldn't be here – but I must thank you for letting us stay in your house. These past three days have been lovely.'

'Where are your friends?' he asked.

'We have all gone our separate ways today.'

'Did you quarrel?'

'No, I only quarrel with you, and you have not been here.'

'Aren't you going to ask me where I have been?'

'I know.' Diana bent and flung a pebble into the canal as if to smash their reflections. 'You have been sleeping with a teacher from a local school or a nurse or a . . . You have a leaning for the caring professions.'

'She was a drama teacher, actually.'

'I presume she still is one. She is not deceased, is she? What you mean is that you have decided that you are not sleeping with her anymore. It has become a pattern – it would be better for all concerned if you remained chaste.'

'I have a problem,' he said.

'I do not wish to share it,' said Diana.

'I'm afraid you will have to, at least, for a short time. It is of a practical nature.' He spoke regretfully. 'I have to return to the house. Things did not work out with Rosemary.'

'It's your house,' said Diana.

'I'll need to share a room with you.' She turned as he spoke. He smiled and placed his arm on her shoulder. She smiled back.

'No, you will not need to share with me.' She gently removed his arm from her shoulder. 'Bertrand is sharing a room with Victor. Kenneth is sharing a room with Betty. I am alone. Your bedroom is not occupied. Did you want us to leave? We can book into a hotel for the next four days.'

'Of course not. But won't your friends be surprised to see me?'

'I don't think my friends would be surprised at all,' said Diana. 'I've spoken with them about you. Betty forecast that you might turn up. And you have.'

They walked back together towards the house, the front of which overlooked the canal. He waited for Diana to converse, chat, enthuse. She did none of these things but she did not sulk. For him it was like taking part in some silent film. Within the short distance from the canal-side to the gate of his house Diana became mysterious to him.

How could this be? He had known her on and off for years. Known her in every way – in every sense – or had he? She used her borrowed key to open the door of his house.

Betty looked at her watch. Another five minutes and Kenneth would come to collect her. She fastened the top button of her coat. Like most churches this one was a little chilly. In spite of this, she had been sitting here for just under an hour. The painting, a Bratby, placed at the back of an altar in a C. of E. College of Education chapel, had been worth the visit.

The mural was large, or seemed large – some thirty feet wide and twelve feet high. It depicted a crucifixion, and to some it might even appear blasphemous – the models for the piece were not taken from history. They were the artist's friends and family and they were dotted in disorderly fashion all about him. The artist himself was nailed up there. Betty felt she could quite easily plonk herself somewhere in the picture. Perhaps she could lean against that pram, or was it a pushchair? There was nothing pious about this work, but the mental state portrayed in so many of the faces was so knowing – or perhaps accepting. There was no story here – just a statement.

Betty left her seat and made her way to the entrance of the church. She paused to look at some of the notices pinned up in the doorway. A girl student bade her good day and sold her a raffle ticket in aid of cancer research. And if Betty was staying in Lancaster long, would she like to come to a college performance of *The Mikado*?

'I will buy a ticket. If you have a full house do remember that you will have at least one spare ticket. I shall not attend – I have seen *The Mikado* no less than fifteen times. I never enjoyed it once. At this time in my life I do not feel duty-bound to attend.'

'I know just how you feel,' said the girl. 'I'm bloody well pissed off with it myself. We did it in the sixth form before I came here.'

'I'll take two tickets,' said Betty, who found the girl absolutely charming. Such clarity.

'I think your husband is waiting for you.' The girl pointed to the taxi waiting in the driveway. She accompanied Betty down the steps of the church, holding her elbow from time to time. Kenneth met the two of them.

'Have you been waiting long, Betty my dear?'

'No, barely a second – I was just talking to this young lady. She is a student here.' Kenneth smiled a greeting and opened the taxi door. 'Such a nice girl. She could have fitted into the picture too – a little blunt, but goodhearted. Did you have a good time, Kenneth? I hope teaching is kind to her.'

Kenneth was pleased to see that Betty was content. She had stated that Lancaster was the jewel of the North, this very morning. They had been here for three days now and had spent only two hours in Morecambe. Betty had complained that the light from the sand and the sea made her eyes ache. She had not been entranced by the waves and sought a quick return to Lancaster. When Kenneth had suggested revisiting Morecambe, Betty had said 'No, the place had held a soft and tender recess in my mind – but on visiting it again it was not there. I felt no tenderness for the place. Perhaps it was because your sister was not present. Perhaps it was she who was that tender recess in my mind and not Morecambe. I prefer to stay in Lancaster with you because you are both here and now.'

The weather had been more than kind. Rain, always common to this region, had stayed away. There had been warm sunshine in late October – and no cold wind. The meadows and fields surrounding the city were emerald green and verdant. The trees had not quite shed their foliage and blazed yellow, gold and amber. The place seemed to be glowing for them. Kenneth leant forward. 'It's the road that runs alongside the canal.' He spoke to the taxi-driver.

'Aye – I know it. They are fine houses. You've brought the fine weather up with you. From the South, are you?'

'Well, we all live in London. But I'm not sure where all of us originated from,' Kenneth answered courteously.

'Not apes, to be sure,' the taxi-driver observed and Betty began to laugh, not at his remark, but at her suddenly deciding to see *The Mikado* yet again.

'I'm still alive . . .' she tittered, unable to finish her sentence.

'Of course you are, Betty.' The cab came to a halt. Kenneth helped her out; if Betty went mad he could still manage her. She continued to laugh as he led her to the door.

'Kenneth – would you like to see an amateur perform-ance of *The Mikado*?'

'It's not my very favourite show.' (*Has* Betty gone mad?)

'I have two tickets. The performers will be so enthusias-tic. We can ignore the content and watch the style,' Betty almost trilled. 'We can both wear kimonos.'

'If you wish, dear – of course – of course – yes – I'm not averse to a little style.' (Betty has not gone mad.)

It had seemed a marvellous and original way of spending lunch and the afternoon together. Bertrand and Victor had seated themselves on a dining barge that began to chug them and their fellow eaters towards a dock some miles away. They could eat, talk and view the changing scenery from the charming little side-window. Their main course of chicken *chasseur* had arrived just at the point where the barge was to begin its return journey. The craft had swayed a little, first this way, and then that, before pointing itself in the right direction. Bertrand had then vomited over both their meals.

Fellow passengers had groaned and complained, but Victor had acted swiftly. He paid the bill and helped Bertrand on with his coat.

'We'll walk back. The air will be good for you. Just what you need.'

'I feel so ashamed,' Bertrand murmured.

'You were just seasick. Anybody can be seasick. Mind how you step down that plank. We don't want you in the water. There.' Victor hauled Bertrand on to the canal bank. 'Don't look so miserable. I've told you once – anybody, anybody can be seasick.'

'On a canal?' Bertrand, after a few gulps of air, began to look less gaunt.

'I don't see why not. You can drown in a canal, fish in one, swim in one.' Victor shrugged. '*And* be sick in one. You've proved it, haven't you?'

They linked arms and began to walk back along the bank. Victor noticed that sea-birds intermingled with land-birds that were not migratory. Some calls were shrill and some were plaintive. He forced Bertrand to quicken his step by reminding him they had a very long walk ahead. It was in reality no more than four or five miles, but if they got home early enough he would have time to have a little talk with Betty before her nap. As often as not she told the best stories when she was tired.

For his part, Bertrand was happy to listen to the sounds of the countryside all about him. The engine had made a dreadful racket inside that barge. But there was a new world of sound out here. At first he had thought he and Victor were entirely alone as they trudged along the tow-path. If Victor saw life all about them, then Bertrand heard it.

The canal and its banks and the land beyond seemed to be full of sound. These sounds reminded Bertrand of some of the medieval pictorial versions of heaven and hell. There were shrill sea-gull screams, soft, sweet whistles, clicking noises, an occasional squawk, then a faint squeal, the bleating of distant sheep, grunts, chirps – and the lapping of the water itself. One could connect a devil or an angel to these sounds. He stopped Victor to point out an old stone building that might once have been stables.

He beckoned Victor to look at some kind of trough he had found. As Victor approached, Bertrand touched him – lightly across the top of his thigh.

They made their own sounds – pain, joy, fear, satisfaction; all were there as part of nature's chorus.

Bill Bluelea was rather taken aback by his introduction to Diana's friends. It took place in the large lounge of his house. First it had been Kenneth and Betty who entered the lounge. Betty looked most terribly ill; there seemed little flesh to her at all. The hands seemed to flutter when she gestured. The tiny hands, the small head with tufts of grey hair sprouting from it – and the eyes, wide and blue, staring out from an emaciated face . . .

'Do you like our kimonos? You must be Bill? I am Betty and he is Kenneth. So nice to meet our host – and even nicer to know that he is not to be absent, after all.' Bill lightly held Betty's claw-like hand as a greeting and acknowledged Kenneth's presence with a nod.

'It's very odd, most odd, but I didn't notice that you were both wearing kimonos when you came in. I mean, it's not everyday you see people in them, is it?' Bill hesitated, as Kenneth and Betty had failed to respond. 'I must say, they look most comfortable – and – er – sensible – and charming.'

'I'm glad you think so,' said Kenneth, who had suddenly decided that Bill was not nearly as bad as Diana had painted him.

'We are going to see *The Mikado* tonight,' Betty explained.

'You're not in the chorus?'

'No, but from past experience of this particular show, I have noticed that the players always seem to enjoy it more than the audience. Kenneth and I will be the link between the stage and the auditorium. Do you enjoy dramatics, Bill?'

'I lecture on Ibsen, as part of this degree course.' Betty felt that Bill's reply had hardly answered her question. She knew that now he would begin to spout about Ibsen – specialist teachers always did this bloody trick. But before he could talk of Nora or even mention Hedda, Diana Glove had come into the room.

'Ah, I'm glad you've met one another. Anybody like a glass of sherry?' Bill accepted Diana's offer but both Betty and Kenneth declined. Bill sipped at his glass. Victor's voice called out to Betty as he descended the stairs.

'Oh Betty, Betty! What do you think? Bertrand aroused me along the canal and I had him in a stable. All raw, it was, and . . .' Victor stopped talking abruptly as he entered the room.

'Ahem,' Diana coughed. 'Victor, this is Bill. Bill, this is Victor.'

'Oh, I'm sorry. I mean, I'm not sorry to meet you. Oh, God, what *do* I mean . . .' Everyone began to laugh at Victor's embarrassment. Bertrand entered to the laughter. On being introduced to Bill, he said that Diana had 'talked such a lot about you.' Diana had glared at Bertrand when he had said this but he appeared not to notice – and went on to congratulate Bill on his house, his garden, his job, and on having Diana as a friend.

For the rest of their stay Bill did not manage to see Diana alone. Of course, he had lied to her about the half-term dates. Each day he lectured and each day Diana toured the city and its environs with her friends. Each evening he would hear them enthuse about sights he had not known were there. He had eaten with them most evenings. He had never imagined Diana could have had such original friends.

Only once had he chosen to leave his attic bedroom in the early hours of the morning to tap on Diana's door. She had not been asleep. The light shone from beneath the door. He had rapped a second time. A note had been slipped under the door from the other side.

> *Bill – I do love you. You have been so kind. My friends all like you. I do love you – but you can't come in here.*
> *Yours,*
> *Diana*

He had crept away wanting to feel hurt and humiliated. In fact, he lay in his own bed in an acute state of excitement. Bill was a hunter, still a predator, and he enjoyed the chase.

It was on the morning of his guests' departure that he managed to find some time alone with Diana. Her friends had gone for a short walk before embarking on the car journey to London. He found her making sandwiches in the kitchen.

'Can I help?'

'You can spread the butter, if you like.'

'I'm sorry you're going – that you're all leaving. I've enjoyed you being here.' Bill stretched his hand to touch Diana's. She withdrew her hand swiftly and received a smear of butter across her fingers.

'We're all sorry that the holiday is over. You've been so good.' She licked the butter from her hand. 'Could you pass me a little of the lettuce and the salt. Thanks.' She looked up from the salad. 'I am sorry to be leaving, too.'

'You never fluked while you were here.'

'What! How dare you!' Diana slammed a piece of bread down on to the bed of lettuce and tomatoes.

'Fluking is fishing – it's peculiar to this area.'

'I'll bet it's peculiar to *you*.'

'Fluke are like small plaice or dabs. They're small flatfish,' Bill explained.

'I couldn't catch anything on a hook.' Diana shook her head. 'The thought of it through a lip – even a fish's lip. . .' Diana shuddered.

'There are no hooks – you just paddle for fluke.'

'Oh really? I love paddling.'

'You have to find the shallows and sandy beds in which they burrow and lie. Then you move your feet slowly through the mud and sand until you feel the fish wriggling and tickling your toes.'

'I don't believe you,' said Diana, who had let herself be enraptured.

'It's true,' he said. 'Shall I see you again? Will you come up again, soon?'

'No, but you can come down to see me. I'm weak – ridiculously weak. Now, would you please butter the bread. They will all be back soon and I want to be ready. It's a long drive back. Slice the tomatoes thinly. There's a lump of cheese – grate it, would you . . .' Bill dutifully obeyed these domestic instructions.

Fourteen

'I can manage the physical pain, the debility and sickness, even the prospect of my demise – but this! This is something that I had not reckoned with at all. I feel so humiliated and so curiously hurt – and yet I ought not to, for after all, it is of my own making. My body appears to have returned to its early state of helplessness. In that sense, I feel that I want to cry. But I cannot. What a mess it all is.'

Betty stood at the side of her bed and held as much of her nightdress away from her body as she possibly could. The excrement – her excrement – seemed all about her: the sheets on the bed were soiled and stained as were her night garments. This was Betty's bleakest dawn. She had called for help for the first time in her life – she had made a fearful call. 'Kenneth! Kenneth!' she had cried out.

Kenneth stood near her. She had expected him to recoil from the stench and distress. He was a fastidious man. If what he could see or smell affected him in any way, then he did not express it. He did not appear to be appalled by the nauseous surroundings nor horrified by what had caused them.

'There is no reason for you to feel humiliated. We had better get you cleaned up. Just stay where you are for a minute.' This was all he said.

It was as though this present horror had been something that he had witnessed every day of his life. And what did he mean by 'we'? Had he gone to fetch Bertrand or Victor? Betty attempted to suppress the feelings of panic that prompted her first cry. She did not want others to see her in this way . . . so reduced . . . and . . . Kenneth returned alone.

He carried a brown case which he lay on the floor and opened. He took from it a rubber sheet which he placed on the floor.

'Step on this would you, Betty dear? Thank you. I'll just pop out for a second and get a bowl of warm water.'

On his return – 'Take off your nightdress – that's it. You can do that yourself. Throw it on the bed. I'll deal with all that later. But you first – could you stand nearer the centre of the rubber; yes, that's better. We'll soon have you in working order.' Betty did as she was asked but felt more like someone being visited by an electrician who had come to mend a fuse, than someone who had . . . well, to put it bluntly . . . shit herself. Kenneth knelt beside her and placed a soft sponge in the warm water.

'Just turn around a little – fine – there – there we are.' Kenneth sponged and cleaned parts of Betty's body that nobody living had ever touched but she herself. She felt no shame in this; on the contrary, she felt grateful. He patted her dry and then showered her liberally with talcum powder so that when this immediate task was complete she smelt of lilies of the valley.

'Put on your dressing-gown now dear – we don't want you catching cold. And I have these.' Kenneth held up some white knickers that looked rather bulky.

'What on earth are they?'

'Sani-knickers dear.'

'Oh!'

'They are not unusually attractive to look at – but they are practical. If an accident occurs again, all we have to do is discard them. Likewise they should take care of any problems you might have with your water-works.' This formal, efficient tone that Kenneth had now adopted softened Betty's feelings about herself.

The tone offered acceptance of her state of being without criticism or patronising sympathy. It was both practical and comforting without being unctious or emotional. Betty looked into the open case and saw that Kenneth had been prepared in advance for this situation.

'A thought-out act of kindness is probably worth more than a spontaneous one,' Betty murmured as she watched Kenneth strip the bed of its soiled sheets.

'Good, it hasn't seeped through on to the mattress.' Kenneth took another rubber sheet from the case and stretched it over the bed. 'There, I'll put new sheets on as soon as this lot has been soaked.'

'Aren't you going to throw them away?'

'They are only stained, Betty. These stains are not lasting.' Kenneth bundled them together and took them out of the room and out of Betty's sight. 'Put your slippers on and join me in the kitchen for some tea,' he called over his shoulder as he stepped onto the landing.

Betty sipped her tea. It now seemed like any other morning. Kenneth had somehow managed to rid her of any feelings of hurt and humiliation about what had happened earlier. She found that she was even able to talk about it.

'Mm . . mm . . ah, that's good.' Betty gulped at her tea. 'You know Kenneth, it's not altogether true.'

'True?'

'I'm sorry, my mind was drifting. I have experienced all of that before. I mean, after nappies and babyhood. It is odd but I have not thought of it until now.'

'The remembrance was dormant, then; painful remembrances often are. It will probably not be painful to recall as of this moment in time.' Kenneth filled Betty's cup and waited for her recollection.

'I was eleven years of age. It was Sunday morning and I

was out with my father. This was unusual as I rarely accompanied my father anywhere.'

'Why was that?' Kenneth asked.

'Oh, he . . . he . . .' Betty paused and seemed to study her teacup . . . 'Oh, he did not like to be seen with me. To begin with – he did not want a girl-child – and an ugly girl-child seemed to make matters worse. I'm afraid I did not possess prettiness or even charm – qualities in a female that he may have liked. "Oh, it's our Betty, she's clever," he would say as though my ill-favoured looks and intellect put me beyond his consideration or paternity. "Don't know where she came from." He would laugh when he said this to his friends – my presence was an irritant and this was how he dealt with it.

'On this Sunday my father had grudgingly agreed to take me out of the house as the doctor was coming to visit my mother. At all costs the reason for the visit had to be kept from me.

'He did not hold my hand – like some fathers do with their young daughters – he did not even let me walk alongside of him – I trailed some ten or fifteen yards behind. His long, swift strides left me half-running most of the time even to maintain the slender proximity with him that I had. Occasionally, he would look over his shoulder and call – "You still there, then – the wind not blown you away?"

'When we entered the park he did not walk anywhere near the childrens' playground but walked along the touchline of a football field. He spoke in a most friendly manner to some of the spectators watching their works teams bound around the pitch. He began to talk to another man who had as his companion a large Alsatian dog. The dog seemed impatient and nervous and sniffed about the turf. I moved a little further away. My father, who was still engrossed in his conversation, did not seem to notice that the dog had pursued me.

'The animal began to circle me as though I was some kind of helpless prey that its distant forbears might have hunted. There were adults all about me but I felt desolate and terrified. When the Alsatian's top lip curled to reveal long yellow teeth – when this dog that had become a wolf began to snarl – I called out.

'"Dad! Dad! He's going to kill me! Dad!" I expected to be rescued. But he bawled at me.

'"Don't be silly. Stand still. Just watch the football. Stand still!"

'I tried to look at the football – I tried not to look at the dog. Yet, I could hear the low snarls and growls – I felt myself falling as some great weight struck my shoulder. There was an alien smell – and my terror increased when I fell to the ground.'

'Good Lord! Poor dear Betty – and were you bitten? Ravaged?' Kenneth asked – his tea had gone cold. He placed the cup quietly back in the saucer.

'No, just very shocked. It was one of the footballers who rescued me.'

'What did he look like?'

'The Alsatian?'

'No, dogs are so alike. The footballer.'

'Really, Kenneth, I cannot see how the footballer's looks would affect the situation at all.' Betty could not help but sound exasperated.

'I'm sorry,' Kenneth added in a contrite, quiet voice.

'No, the dog did not ravage me. But my father did. Not in a physical way. When he arrived, he roared his disapproval of me and apologised to the dog owner. Then he noticed the darkening patches on my blue and white gingham frock. It was the fright, you see – I began to cry. He smacked by bare legs three or four times. Hard, stinging slaps, they were.'

'"There, there, there – that'll teach you to be dirty, my girl. That's what Miss Know-Alls get when they are dirty.

Don't they teach you to be clean at school? You can walk home on your own. I wouldn't be seen dead with you. You're not a girl that anyone could take anywhere." How I got myself home in that state, I'll never know,' Betty nodded her head – yes, *that* was a real humiliation.

'I think it was most unfair of him. But then, parents are often unfair to their children – often cruel. I saw my own father very rarely – but he too was often cruel. My sister and I did not see a great deal of one another as I was sent to a prep boarding-school just before my seventh birthday.' Kenneth wondered if they had exhausted childhood for the morning but Betty was attentive so he continued.

'He was a military man and we moved about quite a deal. One rented house to the next. At my different boarding-schools they were constantly getting mixed up as to the exact whereabouts of my home. On one occasion I even returned to a house that my parents had left. At thirteen, I always longed for the vacation so that I could see my mother. The all-male world of cold showers and smelly dormitories – male-smelly dormitories – I had come to loathe.'

'You spent a lot of time with your mother during the holidays?'

'I would like to have done – but I didn't get much chance. She spent a great deal of time in her bedroom. In fact, she rarely came out of it. My father told us all that she was delicate. For some reason he could not accept her depression – her withdrawal from all of us. My father had by this time a "live-in" factotum.'

'I have never heard that word?'

'Oh, it is someone that does virtually everything about the house. Mrs Bawden completed my mother's feelings of redundancy. She was extremely capable and devoted to my father. It was Mrs Bawden who allowed me to see my mother – usually between 11.30 and 12.30 in the morning. I loved going into that bedroom. The soft pink lampshades, the warmth, the gentle perfume, the long house-coats and nightdresses draped over chairs, the satin slippers, the nylon stockings . . . it was an enchantment for me.'

'A contrast to your other environments?'

'Precisely. My mother would be sitting up in bed. Her pale skin highly powdered – her fine blonde hair softly curled.'

' "And what are we to talk of today, Kenneth? Are you going to tell me about your school studies? Or your friends? Or are you going to read to me? Ah, you do not answer. Perhaps then – you would like to paint my fingernails? You do it so well." She would extend her hand and I would sit very close. This worship was enough for me. And then . . . "Do go now, Kenneth – it is time for me to eat a little lunch. Mrs Bawden will soon be here. I must eat a morsel if I am to survive. You wouldn't want me to float away would you?"

'Perhaps it was – that I actually came to believe that she was, after all, ethereal. If she did eat, then I never saw her do it. I couldn't imagine her doing anything so usual as masticating. If Mrs Bawden conjured up culinary delicacies for her, I never saw them – but on those rare times when she was absent from her bedroom, I would go up there and explore it, absorb the feminine presence. And let it explore me.'

'Explore you, Kenneth?'

'Yes, on entering the aroma of scent and talcum powders, the feminine aspects of it all intoxicated me. It was such a different world from what I had known in the schools. In those schools we were all like the boys in Gainsborough paintings – faces of children but the demeanour and formality of dress of adult males. "Be a man" was a phrase that was often used – but how can a child be a man? That kind of man who is not supposed to have feelings, whose enthusiasms all have to be collective?'

'How secretive and lonely childhood often is . . . but what did you do? What did you do when you were inside the room?'

'I drifted about and . . . I touched things. I held things close to my body and sniffed them. Became drunk with garments . . . and sometimes I would strip myself quite naked – and – and let the garments envelope me. In particular there was one silk dressing-gown. It was of the palest yellow in hue and had copious sleeves and a scallopped neck-line. That dressing-gown proved to be my undoing.'

'You didn't soil it?'

'Oh no! No! I never marked any of the clothing. I couldn't have done that. I had taken all my clothes off and put on the dressing-gown. The feel of it next to my bare skin, the scent of it in my nostrils, caused a strange excitement to stir in my loins. I remember walking across to the wardrobe to look in the mirror but the movement caused the garment to brush against me – my body tingled and I had to open the wrap-over folds as something flooded from me on to the floor.'

'Oh! Oh!' Betty could not restrain the gasp of shock.

' "What in hell do you think you are doing?" I turned from the mirror to face my father.'

'My poor Kenneth,' Betty half whispered.

'The garment – my mother's garment – was taken from me. He struck me about the head and shoulders as I struggled to get into my own clothes. He called me terrible names. I could not hear all of them clearly as one of the blows rained about my head had struck my left ear. There was a ringing in my head as though I had suddenly entered some very high altitude.

'For the rest of that holiday I was confined to my room. Meals were brought to me on a tray. I never entered my mother's room ever again – saw her very rarely. My father avoided me and the two of us rarely exchanged any greeting. My mother died just four years after all of this.'

'Perhaps after her death you were able to talk to your father?'

'No, I was always sent to stay with an aunt who lived in Deal – so was my sister. My father hardly ever saw either of us again – his marriage to Mrs Bawden seemed to surprise no one but me. My sister always maintained that he "trained" Mrs Bawden before my mother's demise.'

'Trained her for what?'

'For marriage – for marriage to him.'

The toaster clicked and somehow managed a more robust ejection than usual – so that one piece of toast flew into the air to land almost on Betty's plate. Betty blinked down at it.

'What extraordinary service! This is a morning that is full of surprises!' she exclaimed ruminatively.

The surprises did not end there – as Kenneth washed up the dishes he suggested that he should move his bed into Betty's room. He felt this would be practical in case she needed help of one kind or another during the night. Betty knew now that Kenneth wished to enter her suffering – her illness – and she could not deny that she needed his support. His love? Betty surprised herself by agreeing to his proposition as though it were quite a usual one.

Fifteen

Mid-morning for Bertrand and Victor was hectic but not dull. The launderette was almost full. Most of the washing-machines whirred and clicked and spun and the dryers hummed out their heat.

Customers no longer gazed with stupefication at their clothes being cleansed behind the circular glass doors of the machines, as they once did. Bertrand had arranged all that – and custom had increased. His clients (Bertrand could never get used to calling them customers) could now purchase tea or coffee and biscuits at a reasonable price. Extra service did not end here.

'Oh, I do like something with a tune to it. It's all screaming and grunting and groaning – that's all my two eldest play. I've never heard this one – not even on Jimmy Young. It's so bright and catchy. Is it in the top twenty?' Mrs Pruett was a regular client at the launderette and Bertrand wondered whether or not it was really necessary for her to make a daily visit. But she always came – each and every day at 11.30 a.m.

'What's it called, dear?' she enquired of Bertrand.

'*The Four Seasons* – this bit you're hearing is *Spring*,' said Bertrand as he poured a fraction more soap powder into her machine.

'I'll request it for my sons on Capital Radio. Who is it by?'

'Vivaldi.'

'I'll remember that – Groups have such weird names now, don't they?'

'He was a red-headed priest,' said Bertrand.

'Really! It takes your breath away when you hear what some priests do nowadays, doesn't it? I don't suppose a priest painted that though, did he?' Mrs Pruett held her eyes aloft and gazed at the print of a Rubens nude that hung over her machine.

'No, he wasn't a priest – though some priests were artists.'

'I suppose you can be an artist no matter what you are or what you do,' Mrs Pruett observed. She held her head on one side and bit into her arrowroot biscuit.

'That lady is larger than I am and she don't seem too ashamed about carrying a bit of extra weight, do she? No, she do not. Not her. Lying like that on that big red sofa for all and sundry to gawp at her. If her husband were around he'd wipe that smile off her face, I can tell you.' She paused. 'It's a nice smile, though – it looks to me as though she feels wanted. How old would you say she was?'

'Fifty – thereabouts,' said Bertrand.

'Good God! She's my age!' Mrs Pruett exclaimed but seemed pleased with the information.

The paintings hung around the launderette and the music playing had been spawned from an idea of Betty's. She had been sounding off about enhancing the lives of ordinary people. Could lives be enhanced? Betty had thought so. Victor usually agreed with whatever Betty said – but in this case it was Bertrand who had been practical.

Every fortnight Bertrand changed the pictures – for a small amount of money he was able to hire the prints. He chose the themes – the previous fortnight it had been flowers, at present it was nudes. Female and male nudes now adorned the walls.

There was classical chamber music from 8.30 to 12.00. Songs from the shows from 12.00 to 4.30, favourite operatic arias from 4.30 to 6.00 p.m. and the last session from 6.00 to 7.30 p.m. was reserved for international artists. This service was provided without any assistance from the Arts Council but Bertrand had received a congratulatory letter from the leader of the Greater London Council.

Victor had received the first and only complaint two days after the nude exhibition had been set up. A young, well-dressed man, who had been converted to an unquestioning kind of Christianity in a football ground some months before, had complained only about the male nudes.

'It is a disgrace and shameful to anyone in their right minds. Who would wish to come in here now? I shall get up a petition to have that removed.' The young man pointed to a naked male print.

'You had better contact the Pope while you're about it,' said Victor unconcernedly.

'Careful, don't be blasphemous. I warn you.' The young man wagged his finger in admonitory fashion. 'Who painted that obscenity?'

'Michelangelo. I believe the Pope owns some of his work. Check up. Now take your washing and go. I will not have your clothing sullying our machines.'

On the rare occasions that he chose to be forceful or imperative, Victor could be most assertive. He had decided not to mention the incident to Bertrand.

Both Bertrand's and Victor's attention was suddenly drawn to the small recess behind the double washer by a bout of coughing so loud and intense to suggest someone's imminent expiration. They turned from their individual labours to see Mrs Pruett gesticulating and pointing to the recess. She beckoned them to join her from the vantage point of her machine. Puzzled, they both ambled over to join her. She placed a hand over her mouth and muttered,

'I'm all for saving the pennies – but that's going too far.'
She nodded in the direction of the recess.

'Oh God!' Bertrand gasped and was unable to say more.

Victor proved to be more practical and restraining.

'Excuse me – excuse me – but could you just pause for a
moment?'

The young couple turned towards him as though
puzzled by his request. The young woman seemed to have
a small problem in undoing the back of her bra. She let her
hand fall to her side.

'I'm very sorry.' Victor's tone was apologetic. 'I'm very
sorry, but you are not allowed to undress in here.' His
voice betrayed a quaver of concern as the young woman
was now reduced to her knickers and bra and the young
man was covered solely by his underpants.

'The paintings . . .' Victor gestured with his hand. 'The
paintings are just for aesthetic appeal . . . We don't want
you to get undressed.'

'We are not getting undressed for aesthetic appeal,' the
young woman snapped. 'It's economic. We are both on
the dole. This machine is not quite full.' With a single
gesture the man pulled down his underpants. Mrs Pruett
half-screamed as he turned and tossed them into the
washing machine.

Bertrand galvanised himself into action and handed a
sheet each to the man and the woman.

'There!' Victor exclaimed. 'We don't want you both to
catch cold, do we?' The couple shrugged their shoulders
and wrapped the sheets about them. They sat in these
modern, Roman togas and watched their entire wardrobe
whirl.

'Well, now I've seen everything,' said Mrs Pruett.
Bertrand felt he could hardly question her statement. She
continued: 'I'd always wondered if men come in different
sizes in other ways apart from fat.'

'I hope you aren't upset, Mrs Pruett,' said Victor.

'No, dear, not me. There's more to get upset about than a bit of gristle between the legs. I am a married woman, you know. Which reminds me that I must get back – my husband is away from work – been to see the doctor about his piles. Terrible things. The piles, not the doctor.' She laughed. 'He's not a bad old stick, my husband. I've enjoyed him being at home with me these past few days. He's been a good friend . . . and not a bad lov–' Mrs Pruett's words faded as she had suddenly become lost in some private thought. She strode out of the launderette as though the plastic bag full of washing were weightless. She thought: 'There's only me and him at home. I'll wait until he's finished watching the racing in the kitchen. And when he comes into the lounge I'll be sitting there in my altogether. Naked on the sofa. I'll buy a bunch of grapes on my way home. When he comes in and sees me I'll say, "Like a grape?"' Mrs Pruett chuckled at the prospect of the encounter – she was still in love with her husband.

'I'll just pop up and see how Betty is getting on . . . It's a bit less busy now. Can you manage on your own?' Victor asked.

'Yes, of course . . . Betty eats more when she is with you. I made her an egg-custard – it's in the fridge,' said Bertrand.

'She likes egg-custard,' said Victor.

'I wish I could do more for her,' said Bertrand.

'I'm sure that the egg-custard will be valued; Betty knows about giving,' said Victor. 'Did your mother teach you how to make them?'

'What?'

'Egg-custards.'

'I never knew my mother,' said Bertrand. 'Diana taught me. She eats them a lot when she is out of love. She says they taste like oysters without the sea flavouring.'

Sixteen

'One for Kenneth, one for Victor, and a decorated one for Bertrand,' said Betty, as she distributed the letters at the breakfast table.

'But what about you, Betty?' Kenneth did not want Betty to feel left out.

'There is none for me – but if the contents of all your letters are not too private . . . then, perhaps, we can share them.' Betty added a little more milk to her corn-flakes. Soggy food suited her better these days.

'It is quite out of the question. I will telephone them today.' Kenneth sounded a little put out by the information relayed to him by his note. 'I dislike wearing black,' he added, before folding the letter and placing it next to his cereal bowl.

'Not all people wear black to funerals, nowadays. If it is someone you know, oughtn't you to go out of respect?' Victor enquired.

'It has nothing to do with a funeral – it is to do with our dramatic society's next production.'

'It must be a sombre piece,' said Betty.

'From all accounts, it is a comedy – set in a girls' convent school. There are many parts – but most of them female. The producer has suggested that I might like to double in two parts. There seems little scope for interpretation as both parts offered are nuns. I have no wish to play a nun. I do not find the habit appealing.'

Kenneth walloped his hard-boiled egg hard with his spoon as though he were an auctioneer disposing of a lot that he was glad to be rid of.

Betty murmured, 'Oh, dear.'

'"Dear Victor"' Victor read aloud from his mother's correspondence. '"Now that Christmas is not too far away, I thought it would be as well to drop you a note."'

'Ah, there *is* a letter for you after all.' Kenneth handed a brown, foolscap envelope to Betty. She left it unopened, and nodded for Victor to continue.

'"Christmas seems to get closer and comes so quickly on us. Don't forget to send everyone a card this year, as you missed Aunty Moira out last year and it upset her. I know she hasn't seen you since you were ten but blood is thicker than water, Victor. Don't forget, it's Barry's birthday on the twelfth of this month – that's George's third son. After all he is your nephew. And our lovely Jean is 17 on the 22nd, you know, Ellen's eldest daughter. She is getting engaged on her birthday, so do drop her something. Her fiance is quite well up – he works at the Social Security, so she's made a good catch. He seems very nice but reserved – but I suppose he has to be with a job like that.

'"Thank you for the £5 note you sent in your last letter – even a little bit helps. You don't know how lucky you are, Victor – with only yourself to look after. Dad and me are going over to Florence's for Christmas as I like the children about. I suppose you will have made arrangements down there. It's probably just as well, as Florence would be stuck for space if you came and it's not nice to have a man sleeping on the settee. Molly says, can you send her a bottle of scent called 'Linger' as she can't get it up here and she has set her heart on it. Dad says to put on his regards. I will close now as Mavis is coming to do my hair. She does it in your own home now. Same price as the shop – but, of course, it's our electricity she's using, isn't it? Still, we musn't grumble, must we? Love, Mum."'

Victor folded the letter and placed it back in the envelope. His face showed little expression and he spoke without his usual modulation of tone: 'Each letter is the same – or almost. An aunt's or uncle's or niece's name is changed – the content does not. It's sad, but I don't feel part of it anymore. Perhaps I never was.'

'Part of what?' asked Bertrand, who looked pale.

'The content,' Victor replied disconsolately.

'Mine cannot be interesting,' said Betty, as she scanned the address on the top of her letter. 'It is institutional. Ah, it is my due, my reckoning.'

'Oh, Betty, no, please, you cannot say . . .' Kenneth's misinterpretation upset them. Betty swiftly placated everyone.

'It is my pension – my medical break-down pension. A passport to minimal creature comforts for fifteen years more of my life. However, as no prognosticator would give me more than fifteen months, let alone fifteen years – it constitutes a passport to short-term luxury. I have never known luxury, so I probably won't know how to experience it. You will all have to help me.'

'You ought not to think of us,' said Kenneth, as he strove to swallow the lump in his throat. This discomfort was not due to swallowing his food too quickly – but his feelings towards Betty had reached an intensity that was beyond his personal comprehension. Betty laughed and replied.

'But you are my family. With you all, I am not short of a nephew, a niece, a mother, a father, a . . .' she paused, 'a husband or a wife.' She looked again at the letter.

'It states that my reckonable service amounted to 31 years, 247 days.'

'Good Lord!' Victor exclaimed. 'Do they count the days?'

'It would seem so – yes, it would seem they do. There is a lump sum of £12,231 being paid into my bank and thereafter I am paid an annual pension of £4,214. You can purchase the lease on the launderette now, if you wish. Victor? Bertrand?'

Victor did not answer Betty – he felt that if he spoke he would cry. It was very early in the day for such a demonstration. He remained mute. Bertrand's pallor had now gone from pale to ashen grey. He brushed his brow with the back of his hand, as if to wipe away some horrible pain or a terrible piece of information.

'Are you all right, Bertrand?' Kenneth thought that Bertrand was about to faint.

'Yes, yes. It's just shock.' Bertrand shook his head from side to side. 'Well, whatever else we are short of – it is not going to be money.' He turned and addressed Betty. 'Not your money – but mine – you see, I have won . . .' He paused and shifted on his seat, took a sip of his tea . . . 'I have won £50,000. There, I have said it.'

'What!' Victor exclaimed and began to choke on his toast.

'It is the slogan and order of precedence of a soft drinks competition – you remember, I mentioned it before. A new soft drink, just marketed. There's plenty of money behind it. It's called *Razza-fizz-zz*.'

'Did you taste it?' Betty enquired.

'Oh no, I'm not an addict of such products. I used our dates of birth to work out how I placed the ticks.'

'And the slogan?' Victor whispered. 'I always knew you were clever. The slogan?'

' "It's somewhere between Heaven and Earth – *Razza-fizz-zz* – Drink it." You see – it is as mundane as any other sales talk . . . I . . .' Bertrand looked far from pleased.

'Bertrand – this is spendid news; you musn't look so morose. Surely, you should feel happy and . . .' Betty's enthusiasms were cut short by Bertrand.

'I'm happy about the money – but not the gimmick that goes along with it. The makers appear to have taken the slogan literally. In three weeks' time – weather permitting

– I (accompanied by members of my immediate family) am to make an ascent in a balloon. A degree of publicity will be given to this event and space has been allocated for the venture on the South Bank of the Thames. I dislike heights and I have no family.'

'What about us?' Victor's enquiry was not without some degree of appeal.

'I have always wanted to drift – to float noiselessly in space – to enter other parts of the universe and sense and touch unknown things – how truly wonderful that would be . . .' Betty seemed as though she were almost talking to herself. Some private, spoken reverie. Some private but spoken hope.

'Then, you shall,' said Kenneth. 'We all will. We have the opportunity – we must take it.'

Victor's response was no less enthusiastic. Bertrand decided that he would keep his eyes closed throughout the flight – perhaps if he chose to look upwards his fears might be dispelled.

Kenneth helped Betty from the breakfast table and assisted her towards their room. Betty's only fear (and even this was mild) was that her physical survival in this world might not last long enough to allow her to enter another element. She said nothing to Kenneth – he had absorbed too much of her suffering already.

In the bedroom, Kenneth changed her sani-pad, cleaned her, showered her with talcum powder, dressed her. During all of this, he talked of a short seaside holiday he had once spent with his sister and of the enormous joy that they had experienced finding and searching out the mysteries of rock pools.

'Such rich tapestries of flora and fauna – Betty, dear – and contained in such tiny spaces.'

Seventeen

Bill Bluelea remained as still as a statue as the grey squirrel made quirky but furtive progress towards the table where he was sitting. His tea, half drunk, had gone cold in its plastic cup. The bag of crisps spilled a few of its contents onto the wrought-iron table. He watched and noted the strange preambles of the animal as it approached.

The squirrel leapt from the stone urn placed near the door of the tea-bar. Bill remained immobile as it landed on the table before him. It attacked the crisps with voracious appetite and rapid movement. Even the fur on the creature seemed to be alive. Its eyes watched Bill as it ate. Bill thought that it would survive this or any winter. It looked more like a rat with a big tail than a squirrel – cruel and predatory rather than cosy . . .

'Hello, I'm a bit late.' Diana's statement startled him. He knocked his tea over with his left hand. 'I'm sorry. I've made you jump. Were you dreaming?'

'Er–er–no – there was a . . .' Bill looked about but there was no sign of the creature, just a few crisps. 'Er–yes – I was contemplating the sundial.' He lied to avoid embarrassment. The study of literature had somehow impeded his enjoyment of the absurd. Diana sat down beside him.

It was a cold, sunny, dry December day. The air was sharp and the light was clear. A good time to walk in a London park. Diana had suggested they meet in Waterlow. 'It is small but full of miniature views that please. A copse, a walled garden, a lake, even a bandstand that looks like a wedding-cake, if you like that sort of thing.' Now she was here – and that was all that seemed to matter to him. He wouldn't have cared if they had met in a bus shelter.

'Oh dear,' Bill muttered in dismay.

'Is anything the matter?' Diana asked, as she popped yet another crisp into her mouth.

'Not really, except – except a grey squirrel has been eating out of that bag.'

'Oh really, and I suppose it was a robin that drank the rest of your tea.' Diana laughed and polished off the rest of the crisps. 'You can be mean at times, you know, darling.' Diana smiled and licked the salt from her lips.

'It's a bit chilly. Shall we walk?' said Bill, rising. Diana linked her arm in his. A cup of tea would have been nice but, for some reason, Bill appeared to want to be on the move.

'How much time do you have?' Bill asked.

'An hour – just under. I'm missing a lunch-break.'

Bill kissed her suddenly. If the squirrel had given her something terrible, now he would have it. Diana, caught unawares, had felt his tongue against her teeth.

'Sorry for the lack of response, love. I just wasn't ready for it.' She laughed lightly and squeezed his arm affectionately. Bill did seem to be in a bit of a state – was she to expect one of his sudden, unexplained departures? She had made no demands – they had all come from him. The night had been tender. She sighed and began to point out things for Bill to look at.

This habit of hers always annoyed him, as it made him feel aesthetically subnormal. He listened to her observations on a tree without leaves, on a duck, a coot, a statue, a toddlers' playground, and a pinched-looking clump of winter roses. He murmured 'mmm–mmm' at various intervals.

'It's nearly time for me to get back to work. You've seemed preoccupied – is anything the matter?' she asked.

'Those shoes are ridiculous for walking about parks in.' He observed her cherry-red, high-heeled boots, now caked in mud. 'I want to marry you.'

Diana had raised her left foot off the ground in order to scrape away some of the mud congealed about her heel. Bill's announcement caused her to topple over. She began to cry. He helped her to her feet. He put his arm about her shoulder.

'Are you all right? You're not upset?'

'No, I'm happy,' Diana blubbered.

'It's a funny way of showing it.'

'Oh, you're so unromantic.'

'You're *too* romantic.'

'How *dare* you say that.'

They began to laugh and walk towards the exit. They paused near the heavy iron gateway. He kissed her intently and broke off to say, 'You never gave me an answer.' Diana looked at her watch.

'I'll tell you after I have taken my flight,' she said.

'You're not going away?'

'I'm not going away. I'm going up,' she replied.

She explained Bertrand's good fortune and let him know in assured terms that the pending ascent was important to her. It was not until they got to the bus-stop that she extended him an invitation to join the group of travellers. 'There is a space, if you want to take it.' He had only time to agree before the bus took her away.

He looked up at the sky. It was free of cloud. There was little wind . . . the conditions were not bad. But nature was so quixotic – would this weather hold? The prospect of tomorrow held both trepidation and excitement. Perhaps he would spend the afternoon marking some of his students' essays on *Wuthering Heights* – help calm him down a little. Diana had not said 'yes' – he wanted to be around her even more now. She had almost turned his proposal into a quarrel. He envisaged a lifetime of such quarrels. What bliss. What had she said last night? What had she said when he was spent of his sperm? What had she said as his head lay on her breast? What had she said as she kissed his increasing baldness? 'If you are going to love a woman, Billy – *if* you're going to love a woman – you will have to think like one, sometimes. Then – you will be a man.'

Later, sometime later in the night, he had held her to him almost in the same position – it was quite a new experience for him and he did not find it at all unpleasant. And they had touched one another in more places and it had been different and it had been good.

As he walked back towards Diana's flat he did not notice that two or three pedestrians had paused to stare at him. These people had seen men talking to themselves before – madness always held a mild fascination for the onlooker. But then, they could not know that he was having a conversation with Emily Brontë. He just hadn't been ready for the discussion until then.

Betty had never liked the mystery of the maze. The idea that one should pursue paths which might eventually lead one to the point where one had started from annoyed her. Losing oneself was not altogether a bad thing – but not within the context of thick hedge or high wall. To be void of view or outlook was depressing. Yet, this present maze was most satisfying and time seemed of no consequence. Darkness seemed to play no part – and the changing scenes were exhilarating. There was little to make one feel frustrated.

After turning round one corner and leaving behind a field of six-foot high, multi-coloured poppies of dazzling hue, she was in an art gallery where the portraits would have a conversation with their viewer. Another bend led her into a mammoth tennis court where players appeared to be exchanging some kind of gifts over the net. Her mode of travel on these detours was questionable – she was not aware that she was walking but she was most definitely moving.

Now she was touring a tree, its branches helping her, holding her . . . but what were Bertrand and Victor doing here? And Kenneth . . . ? Decked out in such gaudy finery, beckoning her . . .

'Take a sip of water, Betty, dear.' It was Kenneth's voice. She opened her eyes (or were they already open?) and took the water from him.

She spoke: 'I cannot tell when I am dreaming and when I am not.' She drank some of the water. 'You are here?'

'I am here when you are dreaming and when you are awake.'

'Ah, dearest Kenneth – what a perfect lover you are.' Betty had begun to dream again.

Eighteen

Bertrand suggested to Victor that they might take the staircase. Victor shook his head in disagreement, pointed to the name-plate on the wall that showed clearly that *Perkins-Armitage – Advertising Agents* were on the 11th floor of the office block that blighted what had once been a beautiful square in the centre of London.

'It's very plush,' said Victor as he noted the thick carpeting inside the lift and the gilt mirrors provided for passengers to make a last glance at personal appearance during ascent or descent.

The reception room to *Perkins-Armitage* resembled a small lounge of a grand hotel situated on the French Riviera. The opulence caused Victor to whistle quietly through his teeth. This splendour, this taste, this contrived art could sell perfume, beer, writers, politicians – and even disinfectant. What power these potted palms, sumptuous olive-grey sofa-chairs, glass-topped tables possessed.

'Do sit down. Mr Roebuck won't be long. Would you like coffee or tea whilst you are waiting?' A tall blonde of 'Miss World' proportions signalled for them to be seated. She began to walk briskly away from them as though she did not really want her question answered.

'Two coffees, please. Both with milk, but one without sugar.' Victor spoke into her retreating behind.

Their drinks were delivered by yet another young

woman who differed from the previous one only in that she was brunette. She placed the cups on the table.

'There, I suppose it's the slimmer of the two of you that takes the sugar.'

After she had left, Victor corrected her assumption and exchanged his cup for Bertrand's.

Their seated position in the lounge recess looked out on to a large open-plan office. There were five girl typists whose eyes wore glazed expressions as they worked. Indeed, their facial expression indicated that their minds had somehow been taken over by some greater force from outer space. The earphones clamped about their heads gave force to this illusion.

Their fingers fluttered over the keys of their typewriters. A movement of the foot pressing a pedal below the machine indicated a slight pause. And then the listening and typing would begin again. From time to time the two attractive ushers would glide through this office (coffee cups in hand) and pass through frosted glass doors to a room beyond. The typists appeared not to see them. The clicking went on.

'What are they doing?' Bertrand half whispered.

'Audio-typing. They listen and type,' said Victor.

'Someone must have been doing an awful lot of talking,' Bertrand observed compassionately.

Victor wondered who he was feeling sorry for – the typists or the talkers. But before this minor mystery could be solved, the blonde usher informed them that Mr Roebuck was ready to see them. She delivered this information with such reverence of tone that both Bertrand and Victor felt as though they were about to receive some satisfying benediction. They were led through the frosted glass doors.

Yet another open-plan office, much talk, only three people, all male, all speaking into yellow telephones. Their surroundings reflected the taste and period of the *Titanic* before it encountered an iceberg. There were three shining, metallic herons with light-bulbs glowing from their gawping throats. There were pictures of women shrouded in cloth and cloud appealing to some deity or other, and a small fountain whose water changed from the palest yellow to acid hue. 'Degrees of jaundice,' thought Bertrand but said nothing.

'Ya, ya, ya.' The man at the first desk was not foreign but seemed to want to save time by curtailing his yeses. 'Ya – ya – mm – ya – ya. Look, these drawings are shit, plain shit – we are trying to sell a bank, not a . . .' The group walked swiftly past the second desk, not wishing to eavesdrop on this crude denunciation of artistic effort. 'How do you sell a bank?' Victor muttered his enquiry to himself.

They were stopped in their tracks by the third young man, who held up his hand as though he were a North American Indian chieftain. Their usher stopped. The man's hand remained aloft but he continued to talk into the mouthpiece of the telephone.

'Yes, yes, well they need a softer image. Well look, you have to make time. There's £300,000 on this account. Just on posters alone and that's just the beginning. Yes, we want some happy workers photographs blown up. Yes, we'll have a look at what you sort out. Don't forget, we want a black in the picture. Some women, too. Yes, well, I'll come back to you later. Get on to Gerry, would you – we want a small motif for this campaign. Yes, a symbol. Christ, no, we don't want doves. Perhaps you could think something up on that – no, no birds. Something inanimate – yes – machine-age technology style. Yes, I'll telephone you back later.' He placed the telephone down and smiled through even, white teeth. 'Could I have another coffee after you have taken them in?' The woman nodded.

'Thanks Angie, you're a doll.' After giving this apt description of their usher, he dropped his hand as if it were a railway signal and Angela smilingly escorted her guests into the inner sanctum that was Mr Roebuck's office.

Angie saw to it that Bertrand and Victor were comfortably settled on two canvas chairs that had been placed strategically in front of an enormous, white desk. The man sitting behind the desk was a well-preserved thirty-five-year-old. He wore a cream suit, a white shirt, a cream tie, a white button-hole. His hair (beautifully cut) was of a pale blonde. When he spoke to Angie – 'Thank you, Angie' – Victor noted that the shade of his teeth matched his hair. Angie left – and Bertrand thought it odd that in this building the men did nearly all the talking. It would seem that the women were merely required to listen.

There were no papers on the desk-top, no files, not even a pen or pencil visible. There was a white telephone and a gold-framed photograph that looked outward at would-be visitors. A lady who looked like everybody's perfect wife sat with two perfect children, one of each sex, ordered, tidy and groomed. Victor wondered why Mr Roebuck had need of such a desk. Bertrand understood that desks for people in such positions were not for the purpose of work, but for distance and defence.

'Well, I have to offer my congratulations to – er – Bertrand Motion. Which of you is he?'

'It's me.'

'It's him.'

Victor and Bertrand spoke almost in chorus. Mr Roebuck stroked his chin as though he were cogitating some great profundity and fixed his pale green eyes on Bertrand.

'I assume that you know why the product has sent you to us?' he enquired in a soft-spoken tone.

'Not precisely,' said Bertrand.

'The product wants the maximum publicity around you receiving your cheque tomorrow. I'm handling the publicity and media relations. In other words, I have to see that the recipient of the cheque fits the marketing appeal of the product. I take it you are a family man? I see you will be accompanied by five other adults. Relatives?'

'No, I'm not a family man. I'm not married,' said Bertrand.

'And these other people?'

'Friends.'

'Mmm–ah–mm–mm.' Mr Roebuck affected a small cough and stroked his chin in ruminative fashion as though he were pondering some tremendous problem. 'At least, the genders of the group are different.' He voiced his thoughts out loud. 'Are either of your parents alive or do you have any rela. . . . .'

'I am without blood relations – if I have any, I am not aware of them. I was a *Barnardo* child.' Bertrand's lack of heritage or parentage caused him no heartache but he did not wish to stay in this office any longer than he had to.

'This is a family product, you know.' Mr Roebuck's tone was soft-spoken but had now taken on a steely edge.

'I don't see how that has anything to do with us. Bertrand's won the competition. You're selling the drink, not him. He's not for sale,' said Victor.

'Are you one of Mr Motion's friends?'

'He is my lover as well as that,' said Bertrand.

Mr Roebuck's expression remained still but Bertrand saw the nostrils twitch – as in animals when they sense the unknown.

'Your personal lives are your own.' Mr Roebuck spoke to a point of reference somewhere above their heads.

'I'm glad you think that,' said Bertrand.

'Now, I have the names of your companions. I'll present you as lifelong friends. Build up the chronological differences – the product appeals to all ages – right across the board. Got it? I can indicate that you all belong somewhere. And *Razza-fizz-zz* has a united appeal for all of you. How does that sound?'

'We belong to one another,' said Victor.

'It sounds all right,' said Bertrand and stood as he spoke. This was the usual role for the person behind the desk, this standing up to indicate that the meeting was over. Bertrand was not going to give Mr Roebuck that satisfaction, nor that respect.

Mr Roebuck remained seated. 'I'll ring for Angie. She will show you out.' He moved to press the button.

'No, please don't. We can make our own way out. The route is quite simple,' said Bertrand, as he moved towards the door.

'Yes, we can,' said Victor. 'Poor girl must feel like a guide dog after a day here.'

They closed the office door behind them and as they made their way through the next office they nodded a friendly farewell to a surprised-looking Angie, who was gliding towards another desk with yet another cup of coffee for yet another man.

Mr Roebuck picked at an untidy thumbnail for a moment. He would make one internal telephone call first – then sort out the outside ones. He fingered the thick, gold wedding ring on his finger, straightened the photograph on his desk and picked up the receiver.

'Hello – Gerry. Yes, it's me. I'm afraid I won't be able to come in and help you with that beer account. Yes – well – it's a down-market. It's got to be the same as usual – yes, group of men – throw a girl in for background. You'll need a sport in the copy – but see if you can get an alternative to darts or snooker. Place it in the Home Counties this time. No, not the North – they're not going to be spending too much on beer out of dole money. Yes, great – I'll glance through it tomorrow. I have a sticky one with this *Razza-fizz-zz*. Yes, the winner is as queer as a coot.' He laughed into the receiver. 'Yes, I ought to claim double-time – no easy deal, selling a couple of poofters as worthy winners. I always thought that they were born losers. I'll leave the beer lads with you, then? Right. Thanks.'

Mr Roebuck replaced the receiver and then straightened his tie. He resorted to this curious adjustment of dress every time that he telephoned his wife at home. It was almost as though he appeared before her in the hallway of their Richmond house. These telephone calls to his spouse were not unlike the conversation of a defensive interviewee in his first few minutes of repartee.

'Hello, hello – hello, darling – look I won't be in to eat tonight, so don't cook for me. No Helen, don't wait for me. You'll be starving, if you do. Oh, oh, – er – er – it will be after ten – I don't think that you should wait up.' He paused. 'I know that I was late last night. Yes. Well, you visit the kids at their open evening at school. Well, this is one of the fathers that the teachers won't meet.' His voice rose. 'Look Helen, don't give me that bloody sob stuff. Save me the blubber. Dry your eyes. Don't forget who pays for the fucking handkerchiefs.'

Now that he had replaced the receiver he loosened his tie, then undid the two top buttons of his shirt. He fingered the small growth of hair that curled about the hollow near his throat. He sighed and smiled as he made his last call.

'Martin? Is that you? Ah, this is Michael. I wonder if I could come round to see you tonight. M–m–m. About nine. Yes, fine. And be ready for a good spanking – I'm giving you plenty of time to think about it. It's going to be warm-up time for you, tonight . . .' Mr Roebuck placed his left hand over his crotch and felt it rise with his erection – he continued to titillate himself over the telephone in this manner for some time. Michael Roebuck reckoned he could sell anything – yes – yes – even pain.

'A luxurious place – real luxury that place was.' Bertrand raised his hand and shouted, 'Taxi!'

'I didn't think that the place was all that comfortable myself. I sank so far down on that chair that I thought I was going to knock myself out with my own balls. No, I don't think it was comfortable,' said Victor as he followed Bertrand into the cab.

'Luxury has nothing to do with comfort, or little to do with it,' said Bertrand.

'Bayswater, driver. Bayswater, please.' Victor gave the directions home.

Nineteen

In that strange, eerie, early winter half-light that precedes dawn Kenneth pulled the duvet cover back from his mattress and slid silently onto the floor. Spectre-like in white flannel nightshirt he crawled across the bedroom carpet to where Betty lay. He viewed the shrunken face and eyelids. Was there too much repose in it? Surely not; that ultimate thing could not have happened in the night?

He reached for the small hand mirror on the dressing-table. (Betty had thought that he had placed it there for some private vanity of his own.) He placed the mirror close to her nose and mouth. He examined it. Yes, she was still breathing – still here – but only just. He crawled on all fours out of the room and onto the landing. From there he made his way on foot down the stairs and entered the kitchen. On entering he was startled to find Victor sitting at the breakfast table involved in some kind of written correspondence. There seemed to be a lot of it. Kenneth spoke first.

'What are you doing?'

'I'm writing postcards,' Victor replied and continued writing them as he talked. 'I'm sending a card to everybody. Everybody that I can remember that I know. I have made a list of people. There are 147 of them. Not many, really – when you think that I have been alive for over twenty years, is it?'

'It seems a lot to me. There are people of eighty years or

more who know no one,' said Kenneth. 'What are they, the postcards? You are not thinking of changing your address, are you?'

'Oh, no,' Victor exclaimed. 'It's just that I don't necessarily believe that what goes up must come down. One of my uncles was very sporty, you know. He was a member of our local Rotary Club in Wales and did sporting things for charities.'

'Oh, really?'

'Yes, his name was always in the local paper. He loved that – seeing his name there, I mean. He did all kinds of things – rode on a donkey all the way to Bangor, parachute-jumped to land on our football ground, flew a kite for fourteen hours from our chapel roof, and ran after the hare at a dog-track. All for charity it was.'

'Good Lord!' Kenneth exclaimed.

'It was when he was going over Colwyn Bay that he was reported missing.'

'Was the sea rough? Did he get cramp or something?'

'Oh, no, it was a lovely day. The sea was calm. It was ideal for swimming. But he disappeared into the air.'

'The air?' Kenneth asked incredulously.

'Yes, he was on a hang-glider.' Victor licked yet another stamp and placed it on the back of a pigeon's eye view of Nelson's Column. 'And I think it will be nice if people get a card from me – just in case this balloon decides to be erratic this afternoon. You can't get life-insurance on a balloon ride, you know?'

Kenneth found Victor's conversation mildly disconcerting. He sought to reassure both Victor and himself. 'Oh, I don't think that you need to worry about this afternoon. The two men in charge of the balloons are experts. They have floated all over the USA – even across the Rocky Mountains if reports are to be believed.'

'I'm sure people wouldn't lie about details like that,' said Victor. 'Bertrand is very nervous. That's why I am here.

He has been talking all night long. He always talks when he is nervous. I just lay there listening to him. I just let him talk himself to sleep. He is sleeping now but still talking. His jaws don't seem to be able to stop the rhythm. If I wake him up, then he won't get any sleep.'

'But you haven't had any sleep yourself. How very unselfish and charitable of you, Victor.'

'I've nearly finished my cards,' said Victor as though this had been some sort of compensation for staying awake all night. He glanced at Kenneth's apparel. 'Won't you be cold? Here, put this about your shoulders.' He placed one of Betty's crochetted shawls about him. 'Is Betty . . . is Betty?'

'She is still with us,' said Kenneth and clutched her garment closer to him.

Bertrand talked on. In slumber, past, present and future merged. 'I won't eat my dinner. I like to talk when I'm eating. If I can't talk when I'm eating I'll piss against the wind. I can eat with my hands. I'm done with your job. Stick your institutional care. It isn't care – it isn't care at all. I've atoned. Your penis, Victor, is like a car indicator – no, I don't want advancement – I do not fit the picture – I cannot be framed. You have lied to me. You smell of someone else. This is not your smell alone – tell me what he was like. And you let him do that? It's dreadful. Do it to me. I have a distaste for obscenity. I won't sit astride your missile. Victor, you're so original. Let's see if we can sort this out without hurting anyone – but Mr Travis if you love your wife then why divorce her? Adulteress? I have been one. Yes, I've known married men. The law says you can divorce her – but you don't need the law to forgive her. Forgive? Accept. Accept my mouth, Victor – accept it. This lady is not my mother. I've never had a mother. How can she be my mother? She is dead. I killed my mother by being born. That's what the superintendent's wife told me. I got stuck and she died. Feet first. Feet first. Dragged out. Dragged up. Pulled up. Push it in, Victor. I want to be born. Pull it out. Pull me out and take me with you.

'I love the lanes. The willow herb gets stuck up your nose if you like hiding in it. I can't hide anymore – I can't hide. Oh, oh, I'm falling again. Oh, God. Victor, oh, God. Victorious. Oh. Oh. Oh.'

Bertrand awoke with a start to find himself with his arms outstretched. His hands clutched tightly at the sheets. The curtains were drawn apart and he was relieved to see daylight and not darkness.

This sense of relief dissipated on the realisation that Victor was not beside him. Had he been asleep or was he in some kind of delirium? He closed his eyes and called out Victor's name. Not once but three times – his voice rose.

'Sh – sh – sh – sh – quiet please,' a voice whispered.

Bertrand squinted through one eye and saw the vague outline of a tall lady. She had some kind of cloak about her. 'Oh, God,' he groaned. 'I must be in hospital – I can't remember what happened. None of it. Are the others alive?'

'Are you awake?' This was Victor's voice. Bertrand sat up immediately and opened both eyes. He saw Kenneth hovering at the foot of his bed and Victor standing just a little behind him.

'I'm sorry Kenneth, – but I mistook you for a nurse. I'm afraid I panicked a little. I thought I was in hospital.' Bertrand sounded contrite and apologetic.

'Please try not to wake Betty – she needs all her sleep. I am not a nurse. Perhaps Victor will bring you a cup of tea up here – it will calm your nerves a little.' Kenneth spoke calmly but authoritatively as though he were some hospital ward-sister who knew her job well. He placed his index finger on pursed lips to indicate that further noise would be untoward and left quietly.

Bertrand complained to Victor: 'I don't think that I have slept at all. You can't think how lucky you are – sleeping as soundly as you do. This day, this flight-day isn't over, is it? I dreamt I was falling.'

'You won't fall. The day has barely begun. I'll bring you a cup of tea and digestive biscuit.'

'What time is it?'

'It's nearly nine now. I've checked the launderette. Mrs Pruett has everything in hand. Now don't worry – you must have had a nightmare or a bad dream.'

'I don't feel as though I've slept. Whatever state I was in – it was not sleep.'

'It was the artist in you coming out,' said Victor.

'How can I be an artist when I am contemplating opening up a string of launderettes?' Bertrand would not be comforted.

'I'll fetch your tea,' said Victor who knew that Bertrand sometimes sought fear and despondency. Say what Bertrand might – he was an artist of a kind.

Bill Bluelea buttoned the top of his fleece-lined anorak and pulled the hood up over his head. Underground car parks were cold places; he watched Diana as she assembled her clothing. There were many layers of it and they restricted her movements as she struggled out of the front seat of the car. In her huge, multi-coloured poncho she looked like an outsize Columbine. He wanted to grumble at her for arriving here at the South Bank at 11.30 a.m. Two hours before their ascent. Unpunctuality was one of her traits – but today she seemed to reverse this bad habit into a worse one. He accepted her arm and they made their way towards the embankment site where the balloon was moored.

As they walked along the promenade she suggested that they take a cup of coffee in the Festival Hall cafe. He sat down at a table while Diana collected the coffees. When she returned she saw that he was reading a book.

'Isn't it exciting?'

He looked up. 'No, not really, but it's not without interest. Do you know Mrs Humphry Ward? Highly thought of some time ago. I hadn't realised that you had read her. She is being reissued.'

'I haven't read her,' Diana shouted at him.

'No need to shriek.' Bill closed his book and lifted the skin of milk off his coffee with his little finger.

'I'm not being reissued. I won't be ignored.'

Bill suppressed his sigh. He could cope. Diana's demanding nature no longer seemed to exhaust him.

'Sugar, darling?' he asked.

'Yes, please. Here, I put them in my bag. Take two now.' She handed him two tablets taken from a bottle of homeopathic prescriptions. They were called 'Lane's *Quiet Life*' and were recommended for nerve strain, tenseness and irritability.

'Do you want a couple?' he asked after gulping them down.

'Of course I don't. What would I need them for? What's in them?'

'Valerian, Motherwort, Lupulus, and lettuce extract, amongst other things.'

Diana laughed. 'Oh, darling, you don't know how funny you sound at times.' Diana, possibly because of the exacting nature of her work, often laughed at statements of fact that seemed odd or beyond her experience. 'I listed "droll" on your good points side when I was in therapy.'

'Therapy! You haven't had a breakdown? I mean a nervous relapse? You never mentioned it before.'

'No – no – no – nothing like that. It was a bereavement therapy group I attended for three weeks or so – about two years ago, it was.'

'Darling, I am sorry. Was it a colleague or relative that died?'

'It was you, dearest.' Diana stirred her coffee too intently as she answered.

'What? That's a poor joke. A poverty-stricken jibe.'

'No, I wasn't joking. I'm telling the truth. After you broke it all off with me the last time I cried so much. I would cry when I got up in the morning, cry at work, cry when I came home for my tea. I even cried through a party political broadcast I saw on television.'

'Poor darling.'

'Yes, and the only way that I could get over the loss of you was to convince myself you were dead. I attended this bereavement therapy group in Ealing. I saw it advertised in *Time Out* or *City Limits* – one of those two.'

'But the rest of the group had actually experienced a bereavement? They had lost some person that was close to them?' Bill asked.

Diana shook her head and said: 'No, there was one other lady, an elderly lady – she had lost her dog. The rest had lost persons.'

'Apart from you?'

'Well, I had lost someone, hadn't I?'

'But I was still alive.' Bill spoke out in peevish tone.

Diana shrugged her shoulders and continued. 'Anyway, we had to make out this list of "likes" and "dislikes" about the person that was gone from us. Then we handed our lists to the group co-ordinator and discussed the dead person between all of us. The group co-ordinator called it "catharsis-time".'

'Really, Diana, I don't think that you should have taken me – er – I mean us along to that group.'

'Oh, don't worry, darling. I was thrown out of it. Told not to come back.'

'They found out that I was still alive?' Bill spoke with some sense of relief.

'No, no, dearest heart. I had far more "dislikes" than "likes" on my list and they would not accept me as a bereaved person. There were more things that I disliked about you – but what had that to do with being in love with you?' She paused and began to haul herself into her poncho. As her head pushed through the hole she said: 'I have more "likes" about you now, though.'

'Well, after that I feel resurrected,' said Bill, flatly. He put on his coat and escorted Diana from the restaurant. 'Do you believe in witchcraft?' he asked.

'I am an atheist. No, I hate mumbo-jumbo. Why?'

'Oh, nothing, nothing.' Bill thought of Diana's reflection in the canal and the way it had spoken back to him when he had seen her in Lancaster. They stopped on the promenade to peer into the Thames. The water was grey and choppy and the light offered no mirror-images that might worry or console him. 'Let's look at the balloon.'

The stretch of water between Festival Hall and County Hall was known by some as 'Peace Gardens' and by others as 'Jubilee Gardens'. On the present appraisal of it by Diana and Bill neither title would have seemed apt.

The day had begun to turn cold and the sky had become a sullen light grey with no semblance of cloud. A real winter chill had set in the air. If people talked above their scarves their breath could be seen. In spite of the awful presence of the balloon, secured by its heavy cable moorings, the gardens held few tourists or pleasure-seekers or passers-by that were merely curious.

There were four or five workmen setting up some kind of electrical sound system on an orange-coloured, dome-shaped bandstand. They appeared to be familiar with the kind of work that they were doing, as it did not seem necessary for them to speak with one another. There were no shouted instructions, no questions – the work was being done swiftly in robot style.

Standing next to the balloon, and occasionally looking up at it, were an elderly man with a religious tract pinned to his back, a depressed-looking young woman with a shaved head and a safety pin stuck through her nose, two policemen, and two policewomen. There appeared to be no conversation amongst this group either.

A flagpole sported a long pennant at its top. Diana squinted and could not make out the design. Was it a red dragon on a yellow background? A short gust of wind extended the pennant – it *did* have a yellow background but the red dragon turned out to be the number of London's unemployed.

Diana wondered what the city would look like from the vantage point of the balloon. And when they were afloat what should she look for? One of the workmen disturbed her thoughts as he began to drill away at a piece of metal. The noise was unpleasant, a high-pitched, mechanical scream. Diana plugged both her ears with her fingers. When she unplugged herself it was Bill she heard and not the drill.

'– d. I suppose that I am a conformist at heart?'

'I'm sorry. I didn't catch what you said.' Diana answered blindly. 'That drill seemed to be going right through my head, preparing me for a rawl-plug.' She giggled.

'I was saying that I can't go up in that.' He pointed at the balloon. 'It's not that I am afraid. It's just that I know that I will feel out of place.'

'You mean out of place with the rest of us?' Her enquiry was sad.

'Yes, I suppose that would be right. I'm sorry, Diana. But you don't *have* to go up in it, do you?'

'You cannot make it a question of choices for me. That would be unfair.' She had turned from him and begun to look at the river – traffic – barges – sea-gulls.

'You don't mind me – er – withdrawing like this?' He sounded genuinely apologetic.

'No, I understand.'

'Would you like another coffee – there is still an hour and half yet and . . .'

'No, I think I'll have a little walk. I have to take this flight – I have conformed in the past when it has been cowardly to conform. All of this has nothing to do with you. Here.' She gave him the keys to her flat. 'I'll see you later. Tonight.'

As a sign of farewell he gripped her shoulder. She did not turn to look at him. She could hear his footsteps as he walked away from her. The restarting of the drill put an end to this. When the noise stopped she turned, once more, to look at the balloon. It swayed gently and Diana marvelled at the tension of the cables. What an enormous, imaginative-looking thing it was that they sought to control.

Twenty

Kenneth had put out all Betty's clothing for the day. There was thermal underwear, fleece-lined boots, woollen jumpers, a long skirt, gloves, a red pixie-hood, the yellow beret (which she had insisted on). In fact there would be enough warmth about her to melt an iceberg if she had chosen to step on one.

The car was due to collect them in less than half an hour. He would dress her when their transport arrived. Until that time she requested that she should remain alone in her room. Kenneth guessed correctly that she wished to conserve what strength remained in her frame for the rigours that the afternoon might present.

Victor found him in the kitchen involved in an intricate piece of embroidery that seemed to be taking up a heavy degree of his concentration. Between Kenneth's deft fingers the needle flew swiftly. The tiny stitches on the tapestry seemed to add so little to the general picture that was meant to emerge. Perhaps it was the toil that gave the satisfaction rather than the result.

'Ouch!' Kenneth dropped his needle and watched the spot of blood ooze from his forefinger. He looked up at Victor. 'Now do I go to sleep for a hundred years? Or change into a frog?'

'I'll get some Dettol,' said Victor who knew more about first-aid than he did about fairy-tales.

'No! Don't bother.' Kenneth sucked his forefinger; the

salty taste was not unpleasant. He removed the finger from his mouth and made a slight plopping sound. 'I won't do any more. I don't want to get blood all over the appliqué. I was just doing it to keep occupied – it's a most calming occupation.'

'Bertrand's doing some Yoga exercises to keep him quiet, so don't feel alone about being afraid of the flight.'

'Oh, I'm not afraid. Not that flight, anyway. It's Betty's flight I fear. I wonder if she will last the day. I think that it is only her will that is keeping her here with us. She wants the flight most desperately. I think that is her reason for being alive.' Kenneth let his tapestry fall from his knees to the floor.

Victor gathered it up and placed it on a chair. He put his arm about Kenneth's shoulders. This was the first time he had ever touched him. He expected Kenneth to recoil but he remained still.

'Bertrand and me – Kenneth – we were talking together this morning. And he said that I was to tell you – to let you know – that – that if anything happened to Betty – then we would like you to stay with us two. I mean – not as a favour or anything like that – I mean – because we would like you to.'

Kenneth patted Victor's hand. 'How very kind of you both. I have never experienced comradeship before. It would seem that it is one of the better things that emerge from adversity.'

'Then you will stay with us?'

'Do not take offence – but I cannot answer. I cannot imagine or consider a life without Betty – at least whilst she is here – in whatever slender form. I'm afraid that mine is a limited universe.'

A ring from the doorbell caused Victor to withdraw his arm from Kenneth. He relayed the information that the car had arrived. It was a little early. Twenty minutes later the four comrades took their seats. Betty commented on the brightness of the day. Bertrand thought that the observation was odd, as it was dull, and without sun or cloud.

Bertrand's fear that Diana might be late was unconfirmed. She stood at the allotted rendezvous inside the foyer of the National Film Theatre. She was standing in front of a screen which was covered by a montage of past and present film actresses. Greta Garbo, Judy Holliday, Lillian Gish, Vanessa Redgrave, Vivien Leigh all gazed out at Bertrand. Diana gazed out too – but she did not see her friends. Her mind, preoccupied in thought, had rendered her eyes sightless. She jumped when Bertrand spoke.

'You look wonderful, Diana. Good enough to be slotted in there somewhere.' He nodded towards the screen. Diana turned to look at it.

'I can't be slotted,' she replied abstractedly.

'Where is Bill?'

'He's gone home.' She adjusted her poncho so that more of it trailed over her shoulders. 'I sent him home.'

'But Diana . . . You didn't get into one of your . . .'

'No. This flight has nothing to do with him. He oughtn't to embark on it just to please me. He's waiting at home – or at least that was the arrangement. But I won't be surprised to find him not there when I get back. I won't be surprised to find a letter saying that he is not right for me and that he loves me and that is why he has decided not to stay. It is his pattern – and the sadness of it is that he is telling the truth. I have realised that I don't wish to change him. Disinterested love – it's come late to my experience.'

'I'm sorry,' said Bertrand. He took Diana's arm. 'Shall we join the others?'

The others were sitting on two chairs, Kenneth on one, Victor on another. Betty was seated on Kenneth's lap, her small frame cradled in his arms. From time to time he would whisper something into her ear, then place his own ear close to her and then let the rest of her friends know her response.

'Betty says that it is good to see you, Diana. Oh, Bertrand, the advertising man – Mr Roebuck. He said that the take-off is to be delayed for an hour.'

'An hour!' Bertrand's exclamation went beyond exasperation. Betty's eyes were closed – it was as well for her to rest.

'Yes, Mr Roebuck's clients are disappointed at the lack of public interest. But the balloonists are now making some local radio broadcasts. It would seem that none of us is good material. The event is being centred on the pilots.'

'I've got the cheque,' said Victor and dangled it in the air. 'Pay Bertrand Motion £50,000.'

Kenneth bent his head and whispered once more to Betty. He listened to her breathing. Diana could not see Betty's lips moving. But did the eyes flicker?

'Betty says that it might be a good idea if we sorted out our seating arrangements in the balloon.'

'What, now?' asked Diana, perplexed.

'Smashing idea.' Victor leapt to his feet as though some shaft of knowledge had suddenly crashed through his brain. Bertrand had already begun to make his way towards the exit. Diana caught up with him and took his arm. Kenneth and Victor followed behind – Betty clasped between them in a human breeches-buoy.

If their exit from the foyer of the theatre had been noted by anyone it was not commented on. The makers of the drink and the advertisers of it could only marvel at their bad luck in having such an unmarketable winner. The less attention given to him and his entourage the better. Tape-recorders clicked and flash-cameras blinked. The balloonists talked. One was a father of two, one was a father of three. Yes, their wives would be watching them on video . . . Tidy family groups.

The untidy family group made its way slowly across the gardens towards the balloon. Snow had begun to fall from the sky. Not the fine, powdery kind of snow but heavy great flakes that fell thick and fast. The gardens were deserted as whatever few people there were had quickly sought shelter.

Kenneth held Betty in his arms and carried her up the steps that led to the balloon's passenger base. He sat with her resting on his knees, his arm about her in support. Like some dignified ventriloquist he spoke out using Betty's tone – Betty's voice.

'It is only Kenneth and I who will ascend. You know this. All of you know this. It is so very good of you to come and wave us away . . .' Kenneth pulled the cable-release levers and increased the gas temperature. The balloon reared from side to side and then rose slowly into the air.

As it floated upwards Kenneth looked down at his friends. The snow had covered their clothing and it was impossible to distinguish their identity or gender. He held the hand-mirror close to Betty's mouth and nose. He listened for her heartbeat and continued to listen as they floated high over the city.

other books by Tom Wakefield published by GMP:

MATES

Cyril and Len meet up doing National Service in the early 1950s. Their life together reflects the changes and continuities in the position of gay men over the next three decades. Comic and sad, tender and fierce by turns, this is a story of survival.

'Except that they are both men, this partnership of schoolteacher and wages clerk might be at the centre of a novel by Elizabeth Taylor or Barbara Pym. What constantly arrests one is not some sensational happening or some showy image but a sudden, disconcerting glimpse in ordinary existence of an extraordinariness previously unsuspected'
— FRANCIS KING.

'I enjoyed Mates immensely. I especially admired the simplicity and directness of his style, and his trust in the tale itself to carry the reader along'
— EDMUND WHITE.

'Wakefield's accurately observed and sensitively written study of characters and relationships is a highly recommended good read'
— TIME OUT.

ISBN 0 907040 24 1 (paperback) UK £3.95/US $7.95
28 4 (hardback) UK £7.95

DRIFTERS

Continuing the exploration begun in *Mates*, Tom Wakefield turns his quizzical gaze to another dimension of gay existence, telling the stories of a group of gay men, each in his own way isolated and adrift in a heterosexual world.

'Wakefield is an accomplished narrator; detached, witty and knowing. The stories are extremely moving'
— THE TIMES.

'Exudes a complexity and sincerity which mirror life and prove unforgettable. Read, digest and enjoy!'
— TIME OUT.

'A writer who observes the mundane rituals of ordinary existence and transforms them into the stuff of compelling fiction. One of the main strengths of this highly readable collection comes from the ease with which the reader can identify with characters and situations'
— GAY TIMES.

'In a few pages, in a few words, Mr Wakefield manages to create very real people and complex but familiar relationships. Stripped of the assumptions we heap upon them, we are forced to regard them differently and in new ways. Even the usual becomes compelling'
— SQUARE PEG.

ISBN 0 907040 49 7 (paperback) UK £3.95/US $7.95
50 0 (hardback) UK £9.95

GMP books can be ordered from any bookshop in the UK, and from specialised bookshops overseas. If you prefer to order by mail, please send full retail price plus £1.00 for postage and packing to GMP Publishers Ltd (M.O.), PO Box 247, London N15 6RW. (For Access/Eurocard/Mastercharge/American Express give number and signature.) Comprehensive mail-order catalogue also available.

In North America order from Alyson Publications Inc., 40 Plympton St, Boston MA 02118, U S A.

NAME AND ADDRESS IN BLOCK LETTERS PLEASE:

Name ....

Address ....

....

....

....